He Didn't Look Like A Maniac— But Then, She Wasn't Really Sure What A Maniac Looked Like.

"Are you all right?" His voice was low, raspy, concerned.

"Who are you?" Alex asked.

"The guy who saved your life."

"Saved my life? Is that what you thought you were doing?"

"Yeah—what did you think I was trying to do?"

"Attack me. Kidnap me. Kill me."

Luke made a noise that could've been a laugh. "Not quite. How do you feel?"

Alex was confused and still more than a little wary. The man seemed normal—if you ignored the rebel-style cut of his light brown hair and the day-old beard. "What is it you were saving me from? And how did I get here? If you don't mind my asking."

Dear Reader,

You can tell from the presence of some *very* handsome hunks on the covers that something special is going on for Valentine's Day here at Silhouette Desire! That "something" is a group of guys we call "Bachelor Boys"... you know, those men who think they'll never get "caught" by a woman—until they do! They're our very special Valentine's Day gift to you.

The lineup is pretty spectacular: a *Man of the Month* by Ann Major, and five other fabulous books by Raye Morgan, Peggy Moreland, Karen Leabo, Audra Adams and a *brand-new* to Silhouette author, Susan Carroll. You won't be able to pick up just one! So, you'll have to buy all six of these delectable, sexy stories.

Next month, we have even more fun in store: a *Man of the Month* from the sizzling pen of Jackie Merritt, a delicious story by Joan Johnston, and four more wonderful Desire love stories.

So read... and enjoy... as these single guys end up *happily* tamed by the women of their dreams.

Until next month,

Lucia Macro
Senior Editor

Please address questions and book requests to:
Reader Service
U.S.: P.O. Box 1325, Buffalo, NY 14269
Canadian: P.O. Box 1050, Niagara Falls, Ont. L2E 7G7

AUDRA ADAMS

RICH GIRL, BAD BOY

SILHOUETTE *Desire*®

Published by Silhouette Books

America's Publisher of Contemporary Romance

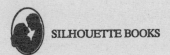 SILHOUETTE BOOKS

ISBN 0-373-05839-X

RICH GIRL, BAD BOY

Copyright © 1994 by Marie D. Tracy

Printed in U.S.A.

Books by Audra Adams

Silhouette Desire

Blue Chip Bride #532
People Will Talk #592
Home Sweet Home #695
Devil or Angel #783
Rich Girl, Bad Boy #839

AUDRA ADAMS

loves to dream up her characters' stories while lying on the beach on hot summer days. Luckily, her Jersey shore home offers her the opportunity to indulge in her fantasies.

She believes that falling in love is one of the most memorable experiences in a person's life. Young or old, male or female, we all can relate to those exquisitely warm feelings. She knows that stories of romance enable us to tap into that hidden pleasure and relive it through characters.

An incurable romantic, Audra is in love with love, and hopes to share that optimism with each and every one of her readers.

To Chicago, the summer of '92 and the power of women . . . Alex, Doris, Olivia and Peggy.

One

She was as beautiful as everyone said.

Maybe more so.

Lucas Stratten adjusted the focus of his zoom lens to center on her face. Her brows were furrowed in concern as she glanced behind her, to the left, and then the right. Her privacy insured, she slowly dropped the full-length white fox coat down the length of her body.

She was naked underneath.

Luke's breath caught in his throat. He almost lost his grip as the camera slipped from his hands. It was enough to jolt him into remembering why he was here. He quickly snapped a series of pictures as she eased herself into the bubbling water of the outdoor hot tub.

Eyes closed, a slow smile altered her features as the heat seemed to take effect. He snapped away, feeling like a voyeur. But then, that was his job: to capture people in their natural state, to report the news as it happened. And Alexandra Beck *was* news. Yet something inside him curled away in distaste for this particular assignment, no matter how much money was involved, no matter how desperately he needed it.

She shifted in the water. Her breasts bobbed into view, her nipples pink and pouting. His body responded to her like a match to a flame. He felt the unexpected tightness in his jeans and shifted his position to ease the pressure. This was ridiculous! He'd seen naked women in his work before, and he'd always viewed them objectively. Public women and private women were always kept at diametrically opposed positions in his mind. Why was this woman any different?

The fact that he'd been out of the country for the better part of the past five years could account for some of his sudden reaction. Lasting relationships were hard to come by in obscure Third World countries, and he'd never been one for one-night stands. He made a disparaging sound to himself, and snapped a few extra shots for good measure.

She stood in the water, a full frontal view that cast all his rationalizations into the wind. The sight of her standing like a goddess in the middle of an ancient sacrificial pool set the pulse in his temples pounding. That, and the abject proof that the wild honey red hair on her head was absolutely, positively, undeniably natural.

Two more shots was all he had time for before she wrapped the coat around herself and slipped into the matching fur boots. In an instant, she was gone, off through the door of her adjacent villa nestled in the side of the mountain behind this exclusive, private ski resort in Vermont.

Luke lowered the camera from his face. He was bathed in perspiration despite the cool March wind. Thank God, he'd gotten some good shots today. Judging from his reaction to her, he'd best be on his way before they ever had a chance to meet face-to-face. *That* kind of complication was something he definitely did not need in his life right now.

He'd call Joe and tell him what he had. It should be enough. Nude photographs would sell millions of rags. He could see Joe's gleeful grin in his mind's eye and shuddered. So much for the mentality of the national tabloids. Let them pay him his money so he could get the hell out of here and stop tempting fate.

Fate was his reason for being here in the first place. His next foray was into Africa, and to counter the unbearable heat he was about to endure, Luke had planned to rest up at an inexpensive ski resort. But the moment he'd stepped onto the transport van at the airport, his reporter's instinct had kicked in.

She had been sitting alone in the back of the van. He had noticed her when they'd boarded, of course. Even completely wrapped up in hat, gloves, scarf and sunglasses, she had "class" written all over her. He'd ignored her through most of the ride, hardly speculating on who she was or why she seemed to be hiding herself away. But then, that old hand fate had reached out and touched him in the guise of a precocious two-year-old boy who couldn't sit still. The toddler had wriggled out of his harried mother's grasp only to grab the turbanlike cashmere hat off the classy lady's head.

If the wild honey red hair that tumbled free hadn't been a clue, then her overly distraught reaction to the incident had. Someone else might have laughed it off. She hadn't, and the question as to why hung heavily in Luke's mind. So heavily, he'd missed his stop and followed her all the way to the end of the line. He'd told himself she might be nothing more than a shy, reclusive beauty, but then again, she might not. . . .

A quick call from the lobby of her very exclusive resort to his tabloid-editor friend, Joe Ryan, had more than satisfied his curiosity. Alexandra Beck, a notorious, jet-setting heiress, had run out on her imminent wedding. It had been reported that she'd been spotted in the Caribbean, but Luke—and now Joe— knew better. Joe had spared no detail while filling Luke in on the lady's notorious past romantic escapades. According to Joe, Ms. Beck was a love 'em and leave 'em babe who had left a trail of lovers in her wake.

Suddenly Luke's inexpensive little rest took on a new dimension when Joe's paper offered to pick up the tab for him to stay on her trail as long as it took for him to capture her on film. Ms. Beck, however, had proved uncooperative. She'd spent her first few days in isolation, and Luke had been unable to photograph her at all.

That was, until today.

Luke checked the film and disassembled the lens from the camera. So be it. His job was done. Packing his equipment, his mind was already racing on to his next project. A small country in Africa had just emerged from under the shadow of its president for life. The old general had died, leaving his weak son as his successor. Instead of a smooth transition, chaos was reigning supreme . . . and no one, not even the major television networks, was covering it.

With the budget-slashing of the past few years, most of the foreign news bureaus had been forced to endure massive cuts in staff or complete closings. This left the field wide open for free-lance photojournalists like himself. With little more than his equipment and a duffel bag, he could travel at will, documenting what was going on with firsthand knowledge.

Over that time, Luke had cemented a reputation for himself as an honest, straightforward reporter. His pictures had graced the insides and covers of all the major national newspapers and magazines. It was a world he knew and loved . . . and couldn't wait to get back into.

He slung the camera bag over his shoulder and extricated himself from his hidden position. The ache in his right knee reminded him of the other reason he was here. On his last assignment he'd caught some shrapnel in his leg after covering a minor skirmish south of the border. What he'd originally thought of as a nuisance wound had incapacitated him to the point where he couldn't return to his work without major rehabilitation. It still wasn't healed, as Joe loved to remind him, and had kept him stateside longer than he'd ever anticipated.

And a lot longer than his money allowed. He was broke, and without a stipend to get him started on his next assignment, he was all but lost. As much as the editors loved his work, they didn't finance it. There, he was on his own. He needed money to pay for his next expedition. If he didn't leave soon, the story would be a faint footnote in history. Hence the appeal of the quick cash for tabloid photos of Alexandra Beck.

Luke smirked as he made his way back to the main chalet. Alexandra Beck, only child of the flamboyant, media-hound billionaire Victor Beck. Wall Street had dubbed him "Heartless Vic," which, considering the source, added insult to injury. Beck owned a goodly portion of the real estate in three major cities...and made sure everyone knew it. You couldn't pick up a newspaper or magazine and not find his picture or a story somewhere about him.

Luke had little or no respect for the man. He had made his money the hard way, and for that he could give Beck credit, but the way the man lived his life left a decidedly bad taste in Luke's mouth. He knew Victor Beck. Not personally, but he had an intimate knowledge of men like him. His father for one. Lorne Stratten had not been as media hungry as Victor, but he had been as money hungry. Luke had lived his entire young life in the shadow of an obsessively competitive businessman who was never satisfied...not by the amount of money he had, not by the women in his life...not by his son.

The chalet came in sight, and Luke ambled past the few patrons lounging by the ceiling-to-floor stone fireplace. It was late in the season, with only die-hard skiers and those who didn't know any better still hitting the slopes. He ignored an attractive blonde who all but tripped him in her effort to gain his attention. His accidental sighting of Ms. Beck had changed the complexion of this trip from pleasure to business. He wasn't interested in any of the glamorous or beautiful women who populated the resort...if he were, he knew where he'd be looking.

A flash of Alexandra's face glowing in ecstasy as she eased herself into the warm water of the hot tub skittered through his mind. He wondered if she looked like that when she made love, then dismissed the thought. She probably had more lovers than you could count. He knew women like her as well as he knew men like Victor Beck. His mother for one. She'd flitted from one man to another until the day she died, always searching for some unknown and elusive relationship that she decidedly never found.

Enough ruminating for one day. Luke picked up the phone and punched in the numbers.

"Joe? Luke. I got the pictures. I'll be home—"

"How many?"

"How many what?"

"How many pictures you got?" Joe asked.

"I don't know. Half a roll, maybe."

"Get some more."

"Joe, I'm done. You understand? You'll like what I have. It's enough, believe me."

"Yeah?" Joe said. "Hot stuff?"

"Hot enough."

"How hot?"

"Nude," Luke whispered.

"Damn! Where? In her room?"

"No, in a hot tub."

"Alone?"

"All alone."

"Too bad," Joe said. "Any close-ups?"

Luke grimaced. "You'll be satisfied with the shots. I promise."

"What did you say?"

Luke looked around at the inhabitants of the main room. The blonde was smiling at him. He turned. "I'm not going to shout. I'll talk to you later."

"Okay, buddy boy, you always do good work. I'll take your word for it. Finish the roll, though, get some action shots."

"Joe, I'm leaving. I've been here too long already. I've had it. And I need to get back. Just have the money ready. My flight's leaving tomorrow morning, and I intend to be on it."

"You're not healed enough to go off to some god-forsaken jungle. What happens if you need medical help? Some voodoo doctor going to shake a shrunken head over your leg?"

"Stow it. I'm on my way back." Luke went to hang up the phone.

"An extra thousand if you finish the roll."

Luke cupped the receiver closer to his ear. An extra thousand would pay for a lot of bills...but what if Her Highness didn't come out again for the next twenty-four hours? He'd miss his plane and be stuck here until he could make other arrangements.

"Nah," he said to Joe. "I'm out of here."

Luke hung up the phone and headed toward the café for a quick, if late, lunch. On his way out, he paid the bill at the register by the café door. Walking into the lobby, he put down his bag and rustled through his pants pockets for his room key. The quicker he packed, the quicker he'd be out of here. As he turned to grab his camera bag, he came face-to-face with the woman who had consumed his thoughts for the past week.

"Excuse me," Alexandra said as she walked around Luke and headed for the front desk.

Luke watched her walk, a studied, graceful motion generated by her very long legs and round, curvy hips. She was dressed in ski pants, boots, and a red fake fur parka with an attached hood that concealed her signature hair. She carried red leather gloves in her hand.

What the hell was she up to now? Luke shifted his weight from his bad leg to his good one, then decided to find out. He walked up to the front desk, pretending to leaf through a brochure as he listened to her ask the clerk about renting a snowmobile. She smiled at the man before heading off toward the rear exit of the chalet in the direction of the rental cabin.

Luke followed at a discreet distance. He watched as she dealt with the operator and walked up and down the line of snowmobiles choosing the one she wanted. She waved off any instructions and within minutes was gone, heading in the direction of the north trails.

Luke checked his watch. Three o'clock. A bit late to be heading off after her, but a thousand bucks was a thousand bucks, and he still had the half roll in the camera. A few candid shots on the snowmobile would be just the thing to make Joe as happy as a clam.

He walked up to the stand, signed and paid for his own snowmobile.

"You know how to work one of these things?" the operator asked.

"Yeah," Luke said as he lifted the camera out of the bag, adjusted a lens, and hung the strap crosswise over his chest. He zipped up his jacket and stuffed the case in the front of the snowmobile. "You know the lady?" he asked with a nod of his head in the direction Alexandra had taken.

The operator shrugged. "Never saw her before."

"She pay cash?" Luke asked.

"Who wants to know?"

Luke pulled a twenty out of his pocket and waved it in front of the operator, who looked around, then palmed the bill. He flipped through his clipboard and came up with a travelers' check.

"Name's Jane Martin," he said, and held up the check for Luke's inspection.

It didn't surprise Luke that she was using an assumed name. "Where's she headed?" he asked.

"Straight out onto the paths around the slopes. I told her to stay on the established trails. This time of year, the snow's funny."

"Funny?"

"You know, soft, tricky. Ice underneath begins to melt during the day, then freezes up again at night. Makes any new snow do funny things."

"Like?"

"Like slide. We're expecting another storm. Big one they say. Last of the year probably."

Luke looked up at the sky. Clear and blue. "Doesn't look it."

"Don't let it fool you. Tomorrow when there's a foot of snow on the ground, you'll remember Tony's words."

"You Tony?"

The operator smiled. "Yeah. Just take my advice and stick to the trails. Get back before dark, and you'll be okay."

"Thanks."

Luke started the engine and took off, following the path into which he'd seen Alexandra disappear. Within minutes he spotted her as she expertly weaved left and right along the path.

The light was good. Sunshine streamed through the tall pines, creating a dappled yellow glow on the trail. Carefully, Luke lifted his camera and attempted to focus and steer at the same time. His years of photographing in some of the strangest positions imaginable paid off as he managed to snap a few shots. But from this distance, the rider could be anyone. He needed to get closer, and revved the engine to increase his speed.

Alexandra was getting way ahead of him, a mindless display of ability. It took all his concentration to keep up with her, let alone take any pictures. After about half an hour, he realized that she had cut through the forest and was heading farther north up the mountain. She was off the marked trails...and he was following her.

Muttering an expletive, he gunned the engine and brought himself as close as he dared. She must have heard his approach, because she turned, and he knew she saw him. With that, she increased speed and veered off to the right.

Alexandra Beck looked over her shoulder. At first she'd thought it was her imagination, but no, the man was definitely following her. Under ordinary circumstances, she would have shrugged it off. Being born and raised in New York City had made her anything but skittish. But these weren't ordinary circumstances. She was in hiding, and she did not want to be found. Not by the press, certainly, but *definitely* not by her father. From experience she knew her pursuer could be the former, but more likely had been sent to find her by the latter.

Daddy was probably well into the third stage of his fit by now. He'd need at least another week to cool down before she would even *attempt* to contact him. They'd had their scenes before when she'd defied him, but this time, she knew, was the straw to break the camel's back as far as Victor Beck was concerned.

He'd planned this wedding down to the last detail. She didn't even want to think about how much money was spent on her exclusive, Italian-designer wedding gown. Running away two days before the biggest media event of her father's already manic career would be enough to make him spontaneously combust, destroying himself and all known life within a ten-mile radius.

Alex took a deep breath and decided to try to outrun her mysterious pursuer. She sped into the wind, veering off in a northerly direction as her thoughts returned to her aborted wedding plans. She'd had no choice, of course. She just couldn't go through with it...not even if it was the best thing for her, as everyone said...not even for the great merger it sealed that fascinated the Wall Street pundits. Not even for Daddy, who wanted this more than anything else in the world.

As the date of the wedding had approached, she'd become more and more panicky. Her friends said it was normal "cold feet," but she knew the real reason: there was no way on God's earth she could picture herself naked, in bed, and making love with Justin Farrell.

She knew people would laugh out loud at such a declaration had she made it publicly. She, Alexandra Beck, world-reknowned heiress, alleged keeper of scores of lovers, international and otherwise, was afraid to go to bed with a charming, distinguished, polished, albeit older man like Justin Farrell? How ridiculous! And it was ridiculous, she supposed, to all who *thought* they knew her.

The sad part was, no one did.

In truth, fear had nothing to do with it. She longed for a man in her life to ignite her hidden passion. It was just that Mr. Too Reserved Farrell was not the one to do it. Oh, she'd thought he'd do well enough when she'd agreed to marry him. But Daddy had caught her at a very vulnerable time in her life, right after the fiasco with the nursing school. After having to turn her back on the one dream that had ever meant anything to her, she'd given up and taken direction from her father because it had been the easy thing to do. Once reality had set in, however, she'd known she'd had to take back control. She'd needed time to regroup and come up with a new plan.

And she had. The last few months before the wedding had cleared the cobwebs from her mind. The idea for a foundation had come to her suddenly, almost an inspiration from above, and once the idea had taken root, she knew it was exactly what she had been looking for all her life.

Unlike her father, Alex wasn't interested in the business of making money. She had a fierce desire to share herself with others, and her feeble attempt at nursing was just a step in that direction. She might not be able to help people one-on-one, but she could sure do so on a larger scale.

It was so simple, really, she wondered why she'd never thought of it before. There was one asset she had in abundance, and that was money. Lots of it. She'd received a trust fund from her grandparents, not to mention the various and sundry childless great-aunts and uncles who had made her their sole beneficiary, as well.

Yes, a foundation that distributed grants to worthy organizations and groups who helped people less fortunate than themselves was exactly the answer she had been looking for. And she would manage it. If there was one thing that everyone agreed upon, it was that she was organized. She had gained great experience through her charity work, as well, and now, finally, she could put all that knowledge to good use.

She had tried to talk to Daddy about it, but as usual, he listened with half an ear and chose to ignore her. After repeated efforts to convince him she was serious, she'd given up. Once she'd made her decision, she had been most anxious to carry it out, but Victor had been so obsessed with this wedding, that she couldn't get a word in edgewise.

Disappearing had been the best way to get her father's attention, and she had taken it. She was ready to return, but not necessarily ready to face him. Running out on Victor Beck was not something to be taken lightly. At the time it had seemed the only way out, yet Alex knew from the first that she would be found, if not by her father, then by the paparazzi who would sniff her out like the hounds they were.

She looked over her shoulder. Damn him! He was gaining on her. She was a champion skier as well as an expert on the snowmobile. It annoyed her that she couldn't elude this man—whoever he was. With renewed energy, spurred by anger, she accelerated as much as was judiciously possible and headed off the trail and up the mountain into the forest.

Where was the stupid woman going? Luke asked himself as he followed her into the thick thatch of pine trees. Didn't she get the same instructions he had from the operator? Luke looked over his shoulder. They were heading way off the main trails, going higher and higher up the mountain. He hesitated, thinking he should just let her go. She'd obviously seen him and would be wary if he came too close. He wanted candid shots, but he didn't want to frighten her into doing something foolish.

He couldn't see her now, as the forest had thickened, providing a blanket of deep green cover. Luke followed the tracks she left in the pristine snow, and noticed immediately that she was making an arc, a slow, almost unnoticeable turn back down toward the main path. He grinned. She was a shrewd one, leading him up into the mountain in the hopes of outfoxing him once he lost sight of her.

Too bad she didn't know who was following her. He'd been taught by expert guerillas in their own jungles how to track the most elusive prey. As smart as she was, she was no match for him. Luke turned left and cut through the woods, accelerating to a speed that was dangerous in the best of circumstances, but now, with dusk descending and an obstacle course of huge pines at every turn, it was downright insane.

But it paid off. He skidded to a stop a good thirty yards below her, nestling himself in a cove of pines hidden from her sight. With the seeming luxury of all the time in the world, Luke lifted his camera from inside his jacket and adjusted the lens as he captured her full-speed descent as she passed him by. Within seconds, he'd finished the roll of film, feeling a bit smug and more than satisfied with his day's work.

Slipping the roll out of the camera, Luke snapped it into its cylinder case and pocketed it. He reached down to tuck his equipment away in the bag. He was unprepared for the warning rumble beneath him, or the aching roar that accompanied it. At first he thought it was caused by Alexandra's machine, but a glance up the mountain told him otherwise.

What seemed like a wall of snow was cascading directly at him.

With instinct honed during years of survival training, Luke dropped his camera bag and brought the snowmobile to life. Desperately trying to outrun the avalanche, Luke careened down the hill toward Alex. It took precious seconds to overcome her. Using all his strength, he reached out with his right arm to pull her onto his snowmobile and hold the machine steady at the same time.

Alexandra was taken off guard. She'd thought she'd lost him, but here he was again. The crazy man who had been following her now seemed to be trying to abduct her. He was probably some enemy of her father's, a fanatic who would hold her for ransom, or worse. She fought him, kicking and screaming at the top of her lungs. When his hand grabbed hold of her wrist, she leaned over and bit him until he let go. Her furious gaze connected with his startled one. He reached for her again, attempting to pull her off her machine. She'd be damned if she'd let him. With a grip of steel, she held on to the handle of the snowmobile as the two machines ran dangerously parallel.

"Can't you see what's happening?" Luke shouted at the top of his lungs, trying to outshout the roar of two engines and her hysterical screams. "Let go, you fool!" He grabbed for her again, connecting this time as he held fast to her sleeve.

Alex broke free of his grip and veered off to the right. She heard him yell something, but she didn't dare turn or slow down. He was after her for God only knew what reason, but she wouldn't go down without a fight.

Luke couldn't believe the idiocy of the woman. Where was her brain? Couldn't she see? Couldn't she hear? He gained on her just as the avalanche reached them. There was no more time for niceties. In seconds, they would both be buried if he didn't act. A split-second decision had to be made, and he made it. With a farewell glance at his camera equipment, he dove headfirst at Alex, catching her from behind.

Alex noticed the wall of snow at exactly the same moment of Luke's impact. Her snowmobile toppled over onto its side, spilling its inhabitants in the opposite direction as it spun out of control before being completely engulfed.

Luke held Alex around the waist, attempting, if not succeeding, to take the brunt of the fall. The incline was steep and treacherously deep. Bodies locked together, they rolled down the hill over and over and over in what seemed an endless free-fall into a freezing cold abyss.

Finally, they stopped.

All was quiet.

Deathly so.

Luke was the first to open his eyes. He was stunned, out of breath. Craning his neck, he searched for a sign of either of the snowmobiles. They were gone. As was everything else. A new world lay behind them, a stark white world devoid of any signs of life. There were no trees, no bushes, no scurrying animals. Nothing. Except snow.

Luke gulped the thin air and blew out a frosty breath as reality hit. He didn't know where they were, or how they were going to get out of here. There was only one thing of which he was absolutely certain.

There was no going back.

Two

He'd landed on top of her, his hips securely nestled in the cradle of her widespread legs. Luke raised himself onto his elbows and looked down at the woman beneath him. She appeared to be out cold. He wanted to check her pulse, but his arms were trapped under her body and he was loathe to jostle her for fear of aggravating any potential broken bones—his or hers. Instead he nuzzled her collar and pressed his lips against the pulse point in her neck.

As his cold lips touched her soft skin, a shiver ran down his spine. She was very much alive, and oh, so warm. The feel of her, the smell of her, combined to make him suddenly all too aware of the position of their bodies.

A picture of her naked in the hot tub flashed through his mind. Luke pulled back quickly but carefully so as not to harm her. Bad enough they were trapped on this side of the mountain. Worse, this wild chase would cause him to miss his plane. He checked her head for bumps or bruises, but could find none. She'd probably just gotten the wind knocked out of her and fainted.

As he sat back on his haunches, he examined her still form and had to once again marvel at her perfection. Every curve of those long legs that had felt so good pressed against his was visible through the skin-tight ski pants.

He needed to be careful around her. She was dangerous to his way of life. He knew her type and wanted no part of it. They didn't fit, no way, no how. This unwanted but definite attraction had to be kept in check. The lecture was to his head, but couldn't stop his eyes from wandering. She looked magnificently serene with her honey red hair spread in disarray around her head in stark contrast to the whiteness of the snow.

Muttering an expletive, he turned away from her. The trail they had been following had obviously not been used for a long time. It was barely more than a clearing in the woods with a half foot of soft powder covering it.

Luke looked up. The sky was ominously gray. He had thought the descending darkness was caused by the lateness of the day, but now he saw he was wrong. Tony's prediction echoed in his ears. A storm was approaching, with thick clouds moving in from the north. As if to verify his thoughts, snow flurries began to fall all around them.

Luke was cold. It was getting dark. And his knee was killing him. He must have done some damage to it during the fall. And Her Highness was in no shape to trudge through the ankle-deep snow with him in search of shelter for the night. He surveyed the area. All was calm and quiet. Snowflakes glistened in the dusk. In other circumstances he might have admired its silvery splendor, but not this time.

They were well off the main trails, thanks to Ms. Beck's unplanned excursion into forbidden territory. He caught sight of the perfect teeth marks in his flesh, then looked at the woman who had inflicted them and shook his head.

He couldn't leave her here—as much as the thought tempted him. It would be dark sooner than he'd like to think, and if the cold didn't get them, whatever wild animals called these woods home probably would.

Luke reached over and lifted her into his arms. She was a tall woman, but lighter than he'd expected. This might not be so bad, after all, he thought as he took the first step in what his reasonable mind told him was the wrong direction.

He was unprepared for the burning pain that shot up his leg like an electric shock. Luke squeezed his eyes shut and grit his teeth. For what seemed like the longest time, but was only a matter of seconds, he steeled himself against the pain. With deep, cleansing breaths, he consciously blotted it from his mind. Shifting Alex's weight in his arms, he began walking again, conditioning his body to function like the machine he'd taught it to be.

He didn't know how far he'd traveled; probably not as far as he thought. Dusk was descending with a vengeance. He was freezing; his feet and hands were numb. He was sweating; rivulets of perspiration trailed down his back. His light burden had metamorphosed into oppressive cargo. When he was sure he couldn't take another step, he stopped and leaned against the trunk of a tall blue spruce.

Gently, he eased Alex's body out of his arms and laid her on a cushion of soft snow at the foot of the tree. The snow was coming down harder now, with only a glimmer of gray twilight left. If he didn't find shelter soon, they would die.

The thought didn't frighten him. Luke had faced death many times over. But it did make him angry. To die for a cause, a belief, or even for a specific *reason* would have satisfied him, but to go like this, on a wild chase after a jaded debutante—for money—was beyond his contempt.

He stamped his feet to encourage circulation and stuffed his hands into his pockets. "Stupid," he said out loud. "Absolutely, positively, the stupidest damned thing you've ever done in your sorry life."

Alex opened her eyes and saw spots. Someone was speaking, but she couldn't make out the words over the pounding in her ears. She was dizzy and disoriented and not at all sure she was all there, wherever that might be. She waited for the spots to clear, then slowly, with the utmost care, she turned her head toward the voice.

It was him. The crazy man who had attacked her. Her first impulse was to jump up and take off, but she didn't think she'd be able to outrun him. Somewhere she'd read that you should treat these unpredictable types with kid gloves. That should be easy enough, she thought. She'd been handling her father that way for years.

Alex pushed herself up to a sitting position, making sure she was a good distance away from him should he try to attack her again. The movement caught his attention, and he turned to her. For a long moment they stared at each other. His eyes were a whiskey brown and held hers in a penetrating gaze. Her first thought was that he didn't look like a maniac—but then she wasn't really sure what a maniac looked like in the first place.

"Are you all right?" he asked.

His voice was low, raspy, concerned.

"Who are you?" she asked. So much for "handling" him.

"The guy who saved your life."

"Saved my life? Is that what you thought you were doing?"

"Yeah. What did you think I was trying to do?" he asked.

"Attack me. Kidnap me. Kill me."

Luke made a noise that could have been a laugh, but didn't make it. "Not quite. How do you feel?"

"Dizzy."

"Not surprising. You passed out."

He bent his right leg, moving it back and forth as he rubbed the knee. Alex was confused and still more than a little wary. The man seemed perfectly normal, that is, if you ignored the long-in-the-back, short-in-the-front, rebel-style cut of his light brown hair and the day-old beard.

Alex stood slowly. She rested against the trunk of the tree and dusted the snow off herself. "What was it you were saving me from? And how did I get here? If you don't mind my asking."

Luke glanced at her over his shoulder. Even now, all mussed up with a head that must ache like the devil, she looked fresh and beautiful. That honey red hair just fell in waves over her shoulders. She had a most alluring, well-loved look.

Now why did he think of that?

"I carried you. Didn't you see the avalanche?" he asked, forcing his mind back to the matters at hand.

"Yes, and I would have gotten out of the way in time. If you hadn't attacked me."

"I didn't—"

A rustling sound behind the bushes diverted their attention. Luke looked around, trying to ascertain the source of the sound. He couldn't tell what it was, but he knew they shouldn't stay here.

He was angry again, as much at himself as at Her Highness for getting them into this mess.

"Can you walk?" he asked.

Alex nodded. She had no idea what kind of animal was wandering around out here, and neither did she want to find out.

"We'll have to head up." He pointed up into the forest of tall pines. "If we get lucky, we may find a cabin."

"I don't think that's a good idea," Alex said with authority. "It's better if we head back. To the trails. It's the only way a rescue team can find us."

"A rescue team? Are you serious?"

"Of course. They must be looking for us by now, don't you think?"

Luke shook his head. "No, I don't think. First of all, we haven't been gone that long. Second, it's snowing . . . in case you haven't noticed."

"I've noticed, Mr.—"

"Stratten. Luke Stratten," he said, then waited for any sign of recognition. There was none. Good. One less problem to worry about. "Use your brain, lady.

If we can't get back down the trail, they can't get up it.''

"My name is Alexandra," she said haughtily, then bit her lip, remembering too late to use her pseudonym. It didn't matter anymore, anyway, she mused. Once she got back to the resort, she'd call Daddy herself. She took a step toward Luke, put a hand on her hip and redirected her attention to him. "And I *know* they can't get up the trail. They *can* use a helicopter, though."

"Which I'm sure they'll do. But not tonight. It's getting dark, and it's beginning to snow again. You do what you want, but I'm heading up."

What a disagreeable man, she thought. He was handsome in a rugged sort of way, and definitely well-built, judging by the width of his shoulders, but much too ornery for her taste. She watched him climb up into the pines. A gust of wind caught her and sneaked its icy finger into her collar and down her neck. She could no longer see him, but she could hear the crunch of his boots in the snow.

She shivered, and she ached. He was right, it was getting dark. Maybe he was right about the helicopter, too. Maybe they wouldn't come for them tonight. The thought sobered her.

She headed up the hill after him, but he was moving too quickly and she couldn't catch up.

"You aren't going to just leave me here, are you?" she shouted.

Luke heard her loud and clear, but kept walking. The thought appealed to him, he had to admit, for a lot more than the obvious reasons. But his conscience got the better of him. It was getting darker by the minute. Between the cold and the animals, someone like her wouldn't stand a chance.

He turned and peered down at her. He could barely make out her form through the maze of pines. He touched the roll of film in his pocket, and blew out a frustrated breath. Like it or not, he was stuck. He thought about his reaction to her, then gave himself a mental shake. Spending the night with Alexandra Beck, under the best of conditions, was not something he wanted to think about. Yet no matter how he felt about her type, he couldn't leave her.

He stopped and waited. As she approached him, he reached out and helped her over a log.

"Thanks," she said on an expelled breath.

He grunted a reply, then pivoted and started back up the hill. He tried to ignore the pain in his leg that had worsened with the climb, but to no avail.

"What is it?" Alex asked.

"My knee," he said.

"Did you get hurt when we fell?"

"No."

He began walking again, taking one step at a time.

Alex watched him limp up the hill. That seemed to be all the information she was going to get out of him. Now, anyway. Once they found some shelter, he'd have to talk to her. Wouldn't he?

They began trudging through the ankle-deep snow. It was coming down harder now. Luke grabbed hold of Alex's arm and helped her along. They had to move faster.

"Stupid," he muttered again to himself.

"What's stupid?" Alex asked.

"Getting stuck out here. With you."

"Alone would be better?"

"If I were alone, I wouldn't be here."

"You're here because of me?" she asked. "You *were* following me."

Luke was glad she couldn't see his face. "I wasn't following you. I told you, I was saving you."

"Before that. You were following me. I saw you."

"Why would I be following you?"

"Because of who I am."

"And who's that?"

"Alexandra Beck."

Luke kept walking, never breaking stride. "Yeah? So?"

Alex grabbed his arm and pulled him to a stop. "You mean to tell me you don't know who I am?" she asked.

"You famous or something?" Luke answered.

"You must be joking."

"No. Tell me. I've been out of the country."

"Where?" she asked with just a touch of sarcasm. "Siberia?"

Luke grinned. She was a feisty little piece, that was for sure. "Something like that."

"I'm Victor Beck's daughter."

"Him, I've heard of."

"I thought so."

"That doesn't mean I was following you," he added.

"Then why did you attack me?" she asked.

"I didn't—!"

He inched up to her, and she shrank back. She was tall. He was taller. He towered over her.

Luke thrust his hand under her nose. "*Who* attacked *whom*?"

Alex could barely make out the bite marks in the dim light, but it came back to her in living color all the same. "Oh. Yes. Well. I'm sorry. I thought—"

"Forget it," he said, and waved her off.

Luke continued up the hill, stomping his feet to get the circulation going as he moved. He knew she was following him because he could hear her footsteps behind him. After a while, they reached a landing of sorts. Luke stopped. It was a road. Narrow, and covered with a foot of snow, but a road nevertheless. He inhaled deeply and blew out a steady stream of smoky breath. Arms akimbo, he rested his weight on his good leg and made a one hundred and eighty degree turn.

He heard Alex's gasp before he saw it. It appeared like an apparition, so close, they'd almost walked right into it. The snow was thicker now, and Luke rubbed his face with his hand to be sure he wasn't seeing things. He wasn't. It was a cabin, all right. A ski chalet to be exact. Not very big, nor very grand, but solid, real shelter.

With a reserve of energy buried deep down inside, Luke jogged forward to the front door. He jimmied the latch, and was pleasantly surprised that it opened without too much effort. That was good. He had very little effort left in him.

There was only one room, with a wrought-iron spiral staircase leading to a loft that served as a bedroom. A round table and two chairs sat in the corner near an efficiency kitchen area. A small rattan love seat and chair faced the fireplace. A weekend getaway, Luke guessed. Not very luxurious, but definitely offering all the amenities. He flipped the light switch. Nothing happened. The electricity was turned off.

Alex stood in the center of the room as Luke walked around taking inventory. A small but functional bathroom was hidden behind the staircase. He turned on the tap. Good. The owners hadn't turned off the water. Made sense. With spring coming, there was no need to worry about frozen pipes.

Returning to the main area, Luke faced Alex. "We're lucky," he said.

Wrapping her arms around herself, she nodded her agreement, too cold to answer.

Luke's first instinct was to wrap his arms around her and pull her to him. He hesitated, then stopped dead. He wasn't certain who would be warming whom. Instead he turned his back to her. There was a fireplace on the opposite wall. Checking the wood box, he was thrilled to find it half filled. Enough for tonight, he thought, and proceeded to lay a fire. He sat on his haunches and warmed his hands as the flames caught and crackled.

"Mmm, that feels good," Alex said as she came up behind him.

Luke turned at the sound of her voice. He'd tried to ignore her and attend to the business at hand, but with the warmth of the fire beginning to seep into him, he gave up the battle and just looked at her. The strenuous climb and cold weather had tinged her cheeks a rosy pink. She grinned at him, her happiness at finding shelter shining through her big brown eyes.

Even now, disheveled, weary, achy, and probably bone-tired, she was a sight to behold. A beauty, for sure, natural, healthy, wholesome. He felt a new kind of warmth invade his system.

Dangerous.

Luke's knee protested as he rose.

"Electricity's been turned off," he said as he roamed around the room. It was dark now; the only source of light was from the fire.

"There are candles around here somewhere," Alex said as she began to look around her. "I saw them a minute ago." Alex found the candles and lit one.

"It's not light I'm worried about." He pointed to the radiator along the wall. "The system's either electric or propane gas. I can't tell. I'll check it out tomorrow. For tonight, at least—" Luke indicated the fire "—that's our only source of heat." The wind howled outside as if to punctuate his comment. "We'll have to sleep by the fire if we're going to keep warm."

Luke climbed the spiral staircase to the loft. The bed was full-size and looked comfortable enough, but there were no linens, just a bare mattress covered with a patch quilt and a couple of pillows. The owners had obviously closed the place for the season, or at least until summer.

"Heads up," he called. He lifted the mattress off the bed and flung it over the loft to the floor below.

Alex jumped back as the mattress careened down and landed on the dusty floor with a thwack. Two pillows followed. Before she could react, Luke was back downstairs, pushing the rattan furniture out of the way and arranging the mattress in front of the fireplace. He threw the quilt over it.

"There," he said. "That should do it."

"That should do what?" she asked.

Luke looked at her. She was standing with her hands on her hips and a general look of disbelief. "Provide a bed for us."

"Us?"

"Yes. Us."

"'Us'? As in you and me?"

"I don't see anyone else here, sweetheart."

"I'm not your sweetheart, Mr. Stratten. And I'm not sleeping with you on that mattress."

Luke scowled. If anyone should be complaining about the situation, it was he. "Suit yourself," he said.

He took off his jacket, pulled off his boots, and popped the top snap on his jeans. With one motion, he laid himself down on the mattress. Luke grabbed the blanket and wrapped it around himself, took a deep breath, sighed, and shut his eyes.

"What do you think you're doing?"

Luke opened one eye. "I'm going to sleep."

"Now?"

"Lady, it's pitch dark in here and will be till morning. I've been up since dawn. I'm beat, and my knee feels like somebody drove a spike through it. The fire's going. We're safe for tonight, and I'm in no mood for your lip. Got that?" He shut his eyes and rolled over onto his side. "So do me a favor, and go to sleep."

Alex steamed. She opened her mouth to say something, then shut it. There was no point in arguing with this cretin tonight. She unbuttoned her jacket and stuffed her gloves into the pockets. She held the candle in front of her as she carefully made her way to the bathroom and quickly washed up. Holding up the meager light, she checked the well-stocked medicine cabinet. Her head was pounding, and she pleaded out loud for an aspirin. Her plea was answered, and she quickly downed two tablets before returning to the main room.

When she returned, Luke was lying on his side facing away from the fire. She took off her jacket and boots and tiptoed over to the mattress. The warmth of the fire felt wonderful, and she flexed her still-stiff fingers in front of it. She looked down at Luke. He had left exactly one half of the mattress free for her.

Alex shook her head in rejection of his offer. Instead, she stretched out as best she could on the rattan love seat, using her jacket for a blanket. She shut her eyes. Every bump and bruise she had incurred during the fall began to pulsate. The love seat was too small for her long legs and she had to drape them over the armrest. She shifted her weight, and in the process, an errant spring poked her back. Great, she thought, just great. She turned onto her side to find a better position, but each movement brought with it a new obstacle to comfort.

Alex bit her lip. Luke hadn't moved a muscle. The space he'd left for her remained temptingly intact. As quietly as possible, she rose and tiptoed over to the mattress. It was warmer here by the fire. That cinched it. Slowly, gently, she eased her weight onto her side of the mattress and gingerly pulled the quilt over her. She sighed into the darkness as the softness of the mattress cushioned her weary body.

As tired as she was, Alex knew she wouldn't sleep a wink tonight. In all her travels and all her experiences, she'd never been in such a situation, and certainly never with a man like this. But these were not ordinary circumstances.

As she lay on her side staring into the fire, she listened to the relentless sound of the snow beating against the windows. The storm had picked up, and as much as she wished otherwise, Luke was right. They were lucky, and they were safe for tonight. Instead of pondering her fate, she should be saying prayers of thanks for finding this place.

She ordered herself to relax. As the tension drained from her body, exhaustion set in. Within minutes, she was asleep.

Luke knew the minute she fell off. Her body sagged, and he felt her soft, round buttocks lean into his. He adjusted the blanket around both of them, took a deep breath, and blew it out into the darkness.

Well, he could now say that he, too, had slept with the infamous Alexandra Beck. He snuggled closer to her, breathing in her scent of expensive perfume and woman. A thrill shot through him.

Luke thought about the roll of film in his jacket pocket and how she would react if she knew about it. Yet, despite it all, his body once again responded to the picture she'd made.

This was a hell of a spot to be in, he thought as he unconsciously inched closer to her.

One hell of a spot.

Three

———

Alex was having the nicest dream. It was a clear summer day, the sky above a blue so vivid it hurt the eyes. She sunk into the soft cushions of the lounge and basked in the sun. She was at the beach, and the waves were lapping against the shore. A cool breeze soothed her burning skin, and she lifted her face to catch it. As she snuggled to nestle herself deeper into the lounge, the strangest thing happened.

The cushion began to move.

With the greatest care, Alex opened one eye, then the other. Just as she suspected. The air was chilled, not warm at all. She wasn't at the beach, and her head was definitely not resting on a cushion.

It was resting on *him*.

A moment of immediate panic quickly subsided. He was a stranger, but, she rationalized, everything was relative. Could you truly call someone a stranger after sharing a bed with them? Other than being extremely cantankerous, he had behaved like a gentleman. Even so, he wasn't at all like any of the men she knew. The wisest course of action would be to stay clear of him until she could be absolutely sure who and what he was. She remained motionless for a long moment, trying to decide what to do.

His scent filled her senses. He didn't even *smell* like any of the men she knew. There was no trace of designer cologne, no artifice of any kind. He smelled like ... well, a man, which wasn't altogether unpleasant, but under the circumstances was more than a little daunting.

With excruciating slowness, Alexandra tilted her head back to get a better look at him. His chest rose and fell with his slow, even breathing. Inch by stealthy inch, she slid away from him. He never moved a muscle, and his breathing remained constant. She was just about to roll away off the mattress when an arm shot out and wrapped itself around her waist, hugging her into his body. He mumbled something, swallowed audibly, then sighed before falling back to sleep.

Alexandra stared in disbelief, their faces only inches from each other. She didn't know whether to push away or start slithering all over again. She studied him as she tried to make up her mind. In the light of day, she could get a better look at him. His hair was light brown, with a few streaks of blond, thick and a bit unruly. He had high cheekbones, a strong jaw, and a full bottom lip.

There was a world-weary look to his face, and she couldn't help but wonder how it had gotten there. Suncreased laugh lines around his eyes must mean he smiled sometimes, though she had yet to see one. She remembered the tawny eyes that were hidden behind lids decorated with the longest, lushest lashes she had ever seen on a man. Or a woman, for that matter.

All in all, she had to agree with her first opinion. He was ruggedly handsome—whiskers and all—and he did seem normal...whatever that was nowadays. Perhaps he was telling the truth. Perhaps he hadn't been following her, only out for a ride himself when the unexpected happened. What difference did it make, anyway? she asked herself. Within hours, they would be rescued, she was sure of that, and this would just be a small interlude that they both would soon forget.

Strangely, the thought didn't sit well with her. She harbored a sense of anticipation lying here next to him, as if she were waiting for something, something new, unimaginable, and just out of reach.

His arm tightened around her, pulling her closer to him. Their bodies had been flush up against each other, but now they were touching in every strategically intimate place. What was confusing was the ambivalence she felt at being pressed against him like this. She didn't know him—didn't want to—but there was something about being wrapped in his arms that made her stomach churn and her heartbeat accelerate. Yet in some ways, it also calmed her, made her feel...safe.

Odd, she thought. Safe was not a word she generally used when referring to men. She dismissed the thought as an aberration due, no doubt, to this unusual situation that was making her less than rational. Alex attempted to move, then changed her mind. She couldn't figure out a way to do so without rousing him—or worse, considering the position of their bodies.

As if Luke could read her mind, his hand began to travel down her back, slowly making its way to the base of her spine. There it stopped, and Alexandra held herself stone-still, waiting, anticipating its next move. It didn't disappoint her. Slowly, steadily, the hand moved to the curve of her buttocks, where it rested, caressed, then cupped her bottom.

The feeling of safety dissipated instantly, but in its place was a totally different one. His touch was warm, while the room was cold, and his body radiated a heat that beckoned her closer. She felt the goose bumps rise on her flesh. His warmth seeped into her as his hand continued to massage her. A fluttering began in the pit of her stomach, from fear or excitement, she couldn't be sure.

Her arm was pinned under his, but she managed to wiggle her hand free. She attempted to push up against his chest in protest. It seemed the wise thing to do, but was to no avail as she met a wall of hard muscle that didn't give an inch. His blue flannel shirt gaped open, revealing a gray T-shirt underneath. Her palm was splayed over his heart. Its steady beat kept time with her own.

She shut her eyes, trying to decide whether to lie calmly in his arms in hopes he would just roll over, and she could escape...or follow her first instinct and bring her knee up full force to put an immediate end to the situation.

She didn't have to do either.

Luke awoke. Disoriented, he stared at her for the longest moment. At first he couldn't place where he was or with whom. He'd awakened in some strange places in his life, so this didn't completely throw him. Realization came gradually, in steps, beginning with who she was all the way to what he was holding in the palm of his hand.

"Sorry," he said, and released her immediately.

Alex lost no time. She scrambled off the makeshift bed. Unfortunately, there wasn't very far to go. She glanced over at him. He was sitting up in the center of the mattress running a hand through his tousled hair. He filled the area completely, making Alex wonder how she'd ever shared such a small space with such a large man.

Her hands tightly clenched, she was unbelievably nervous at being cooped up with someone as thoroughly masculine as Luke Stratten. He rose, slipped into his boots, and headed off in the direction of the bathroom. She turned her back to him and scanned the kitchen area, hoping to regroup.

The pipes groaned their displeasure as she tested the tap, but finally belched out a rusty reserve of water. As she let it run to clear, her eyes zeroed in on the automatic coffeemaker that sat catercorner on the counter. She would give all she owned for a cup of coffee right now.

"Check in the cabinets," Luke said as he returned to the main room. "There might be something."

Luke tested his knee. The stiffness wasn't going away. It seemed he'd done more damage in the fall than he'd thought. It hurt like hell.

Alex found not only an unopen can of coffee, but a box of saltines, peanut butter, and several other canned goods, as well. "Oh, look!" she said, pointing to the supplies.

"At least we won't starve," Luke said.

He was standing behind her when she turned.

"We won't be here long enough to worry about that," she said.

"No?"

"They must know we're missing by now."

Luke shook his head and moved toward the window. The snow was still coming down, huge, heavy, March snowflakes laden with moisture. The trees and bushes were bent over with the unwelcome burden.

"Take a look at the sky," he said. "This storm's far from over. They aren't going to send helicopters out looking for us until that sky is clear."

Alex bit her lip. She didn't like what he was saying. Being stranded overnight with him was one thing. Being stranded indefinitely was quite something else. She moved to the window and stood next to him.

"Can't we try to get back on our own?" she asked.

Luke looked at her incredulously. "No."

"Why not?"

"Because we won't make it."

"Says who?"

"Says me."

"And what makes you such an authority?" Alex asked, hand on hip.

"I know a bit about survival training." He answered calmly, though his blood was beginning to boil.

"Well, so do I. Maybe I'll just go by myself."

Spoiled little brat, he thought, unable and unwilling to understand what was right under her nose. Bad enough he'd had to follow her, missing his plane in the process, now he was stuck spending time with a pampered princess who probably couldn't boil water.

Exasperated, Luke brushed past her and pulled at the door. It was iced, but a few pounds of his fist against the frame, and it came loose. He swung the door open, and a pile of snow fell into the threshold of the cabin.

"Be my guest, Miss Beck," he said as he extended his hand toward the exit.

Alexandra felt as if her heart had just dropped to her feet. There was no exit, no path, no anything. Just snow. Everywhere.

She swallowed, then gave him a weak apologetic grin. "We really are stuck here, aren't we?" she said softly.

"Now you get the picture."

"For how long?"

"As long as it takes."

Luke shrugged into his jacket and picked a shovel off the back wall.

"What are you doing?" Alex asked.

He began clearing a path. "We need more wood. I'll check around to see if there's a supply out back."

With the door open, it was very cold. The room had been chilled before, but now, with the wind blowing through, it was fast becoming a refrigerator. Alex stood and shivered with the coffee can in her hand.

"Why don't you make yourself useful?" Luke said as he cleared the doorway.

"What do you want me to do?"

"For starters, pump up the fire. Finish the logs in that box." He moved to shut the door behind him. "And make the coffee."

"Make the—?" The door was shut, and he was gone. Alex looked down at the coffee can in her hand and sighed.

"And how am I supposed to do *that?*"

She knew how to make coffee, of course, but with a coffeepot and a stove, or an automatic coffeemaker, not with a can and a fire. Determined not to let him intimidate her, she searched through the drawers for a can opener.

Luke began shoveling in earnest, despite aching muscles from spending the night on a tiny bed with a beautiful woman in a cramped position. His mind was racing, consumed with totally unrelated thoughts. Thoughts about his lost equipment, about his missed assignment, and most of all, thoughts about Alex.

He stopped and leaned against the corner of the cabin. He didn't get much sleep with Alex's body tucked tightly against his all night. He'd doze, then awaken to find her leg thrown over his, her arm across his chest, her hand on his thigh. It seemed Ms. Beck was a restless sleeper.

It had been most uncomfortable...and most disturbing. She was many things to him—spoiled, aimless, selfish—but despite it all, he couldn't deny that he was physically very attracted to her. He hadn't had any meaningful relationships in a very long time. Only once had he even come close to getting engaged, and that had been years ago, in college, when he hadn't known any better.

Once he'd chosen his career, all that had changed. There was no place in his life for commitment to any one woman. When all was said and done, even the most liberated of them wanted a house in the country with a white picket fence, when all he wanted was the freedom to go off and cover whatever breaking story was current and vital.

Women and a career just didn't mix. And even if they did, Alexandra Beck would be the last woman he'd choose. If he were looking—which he wasn't—it would be for someone with substance, someone with purpose, someone who cared for more than the condition of her latest manicure. He pictured Alex standing with her hand on her hip demanding that they return to the trails.

Brat, he thought. Spoiled little princess. But then the picture changed to the one that was indelibly imprinted on the negative of his mind—Alex in the hot tub, her face glowing in ecstasy.

Luke picked up the shovel and started working again. With strength born of frustration, he dug deeply and sharply into the heavy, wet snow. Maybe he didn't like her, but he sure as hell couldn't deny that he wanted to make love with her.

This was definitely his most pressing problem. It was clear to him, if not to her, that they would probably have to spend another night, maybe two, together. It bothered him that he didn't know how he was going to handle it. He, who had always prided himself on his self-control, seemed to have very little when it came to Alexandra.

Not that she returned the attraction. She eyed him like Bambi facing a burly hunter. She was wary of him, and rightly so. If he was smart, he'd play on her natural reserve to keep her at arm's length from him. Hell, forget arm's length. Another night like the last one and he'd need a ten-foot pole.

A half cord of wood was stacked several yards behind the cabin. After muttering a quick prayer of thanks, Luke proceeded to investigate the perimeter of the cabin to see what else he could find. A large propane gas tank was propped against the back wall. The gauge registered almost on "E," but not quite. He turned the knob and heard the gentle hiss of gas leak into the pipes. He assumed the water heater was on the other side of this wall in the closet behind the spiral staircase. Luke figured with judicious rationing, they would at least have access to hot water and use of the stove.

He filled his arms with wood and trudged back to the front door. He dropped the load, then returned for several more. Swinging the door open, he threw in an armful of logs. The abruptness of his entrance surprised Alex, and she burned herself on the heavy pot she'd been lifting off the grate.

"Oh!" she exclaimed, and brought her hand to her mouth.

Luke hurried over to her. "What happened?"

"I—I was making coffee. *Trying* to make coffee, that is. You surprised me. I burned my hand."

"Let me see," Luke said, and took hold of her right hand. The palm was red and pouting. "Come on."

Alex followed him. She didn't have a choice. He pulled her hand, along with the rest of her, toward the door and outside onto the threshold.

"What—?"

"Cold is the best remedy for a burn," he said in a tone that brooked no dissent.

"It's not that bad—"

He shoved her hand into the nearest pile of snow.

Together they stood, leaning over the snow pile with Luke holding Alex's right wrist firmly in place. Large wet snowflakes drifted down onto them, and soon, both were covered. For the longest time they stood silently, Alex looking one way, Luke another, both desperately trying to avoid eye contact.

It was not to be. Alex shifted her weight from one foot to the other, and in the process, she slipped. She reached out for him. Automatically, Luke's arm shot out and grabbed her from behind. He pulled her to his body for support, and her head fell back against his shoulder.

Their eyes met and held. Luke looked down at her and groaned inwardly. She was nervous, he could feel it in the trembling of her body against his. Her brown eyes were wide open, and the blush on her cheeks only heightened her appeal. She looked so tempting, like a sugarcoated morsel of candy. And Lord knew that spending hours lying next to her in the dark had given him one hell of a sweet tooth.

All the images he held of her, all the preconceived notions of who she was, vanished in the cold air like vapors of breath. There was an innocence about her that defied logic, defied reality, defied what had ever been said or written about her. But despite all he knew to be fact, he couldn't deny that something had changed between yesterday and today. She wasn't just an assignment anymore, a means to an end, a row of dollar signs. She was a flesh-and-blood woman, one he could touch, smell, feel, one who elicited a response in him that professional courtesans from the far reaches of the world had never been able to do.

His gaze centered on her mouth. Her lips were parted. The invitation was there, whether she knew it or not. Without thought of the consequences, without coherent thought at all, Luke lowered his head to hers.

Panic gripped Alex's insides. He was going to kiss her! Did she want him to? There was no time for decision-making, in milliseconds his lips would be on hers. She could feel his warm breath mingling with her own. Her stomach did a flip-flop, and a spiral of heat zeroed down to the center of her being. Her hand tightened on his arm.

"I—I think it's all right now," she said, the words almost lost in his mouth.

"Hmm?"

"My hand," she said. "It's all right now."

Luke stared at her for the longest moment, then blinked, attempting, if not succeeding, to remember what it was he had been doing in the first place. It all came back to him, and he pulled her hand out of the snow pile for inspection.

She was right. The redness was now pinkish, and the swelling was gone. He looked back down at her upturned face. The wariness was back, and thank God for it. What had come over him? He had been just about to kiss her! He shook his head and backed away from her. Luke Stratten carried away by some unknown force over which he had no control. Who would think it? Joe would laugh out loud. Not a soul he knew would believe it. Least of all himself.

"You're freezing," Luke said, realizing for the first time that she was wearing only her sweater. "Come on."

He opened the door and ushered her inside. His gaze roamed over the room quickly. Their "bed" was neatly made, and the fire was roaring. The culprit pot was sitting on the slate fireplace step. So she wasn't as helpless as he'd thought. Chalk one up for Her Highness.

He turned to her. "There's a propane tank out back with probably enough in it to supply us with hot water, and if we're careful—" he pointed to the stove "—some cooking time. But no heat. I'm afraid we'll have to make do with the fireplace."

"We're lucky to have that much," Alex said.

"You got that right."

Luke ambled over to the fireplace and checked what she had done. Steam streamed out of the pot, and the aroma of coffee, while not the best he'd ever inhaled, sure as hell made his mouth water. He scooped a mug of coffee out of the pot, and took a sip. If you discounted the grounds, which couldn't be helped, it was good. Damned good. He hid his surprise.

"How is it?" she asked, hovering nearby.

"Not bad," he answered, concentrating his attention toward the cup instead of her face. He couldn't look at her right now, didn't dare, for fear she'd see what was in his eyes. And what *is* in your eyes, Stratten? he asked himself. Respect? Desire? Fear?

A bit of each, no doubt.

Alex moved toward him cautiously. She dropped to her knees beside him, dipped a mug into the pot and helped herself to some coffee—all without taking her eyes from Luke's very serious face.

She couldn't figure him out. There was something about him that disturbed her. He was aloof and downright ornery most of the time, yet on occasion she would catch him staring at her with the oddest look on his face . . . as if he were in pain.

Maybe it was his leg he was thinking about and not her. She couldn't be sure. She only knew that her instincts were never wrong, and her instincts told her that there was more to this man than met the eye.

She didn't know how long they had left together, but there wasn't much else to do, was there? And it would certainly kill time, something of which they had plenty. Why not scratch the surface of Luke Stratten and see what she could find? It might be an interesting diversion. After all, she had nothing to lose.

Did she?

Four

———

"**W**hy don't you like me?"

Luke's hand stilled as the mug reached his lips. He took a mouthful of coffee and studied her over the rim for a long moment.

He swallowed. "What makes you think I don't like you?"

"Your attitude, for one," she said, and proceeded to sit yoga-style across from him. "You've been hostile from the first."

"Hostile?"

"Angry. As if the avalanche was my fault."

"It wasn't anyone's fault. If I seem angry, it's because I'm supposed to be boarding a plane for Africa—" he checked his watch "—right about now."

"Africa? How wonderful! A holiday?"

Why did he tell her that? "No, uh, more like a job."

"What do you do?" she asked, sipping at the same time.

"Write." It seemed closest to the whole truth. He did write the copy for his photographs.

Alexandra smiled. "A writer. That explains it."

"Explains what?"

She pointed to him. "That scruffy, disenchanted look you have."

"Scruffy? I'm scruffy?"

"Well, not *scruffy,* exactly, not like in unkempt, but you know . . . messy."

"Messy." Somehow he felt there must be a compliment buried somewhere in here if he would just hang in there long enough.

"Yes. Irreverent. Like you don't give a care about what people think of you. Kind of an independent cuss."

"And that's good?"

"I like it," Alex said with a shrug.

"You do? Why?"

"Oh, I don't know. Most men would be taking advantage of a situation like this. Trying to impress me and all."

"Men do that with you?"

"All the time."

"A lot of men?"

Alex's eyes narrowed. He was getting into rumor territory, and she wasn't sure she liked the direction the conversation was taking. "Enough."

"How many's enough?" Luke asked, wondering why he was pursuing a subject he'd already heard more about than he'd ever wanted to know.

"Don't you read the tabloids? Thousands."

She was riled. That was good, or so he thought. "I've never met anyone who's had thousands of lovers."

"Then you've led a sheltered life. I know hundreds."

"Hundreds and thousands. My, my, Ms. Beck, you have been around, haven't you?"

"And then some."

"I wonder what it feels like?" he asked, almost rhetorically.

Alex had had enough. She jumped up and dumped the remaining drops of her coffee into the fire. The liquid sizzled as it hit the flames, much like her temper was sizzling with this ridiculous conversation. He was like all the others, interested only in the shell, not in the person underneath. Well, what did she expect?

"My experience with men *in general* is that they are greedy, money-hungry users who only care to satisfy what they consider their two most important human needs—both of which just happen to be located below their waists—their pockets and their—"

Luke stood. "I get the picture."

They faced each other, one examining the other, trying to decide whether to end this or go on. Luke had been baiting her, he'd admit it to himself if not to her. For some primal reason he wanted to hear her say the words. He wanted to hear all about her lurid little sex life from her very own lips... those gorgeous, plump, ripe, pouting lips that he just wanted to devour.

"Truce," he said instead, and stuck out his hand. "After all, I'm not one of *them*. You said so yourself."

"You're still a man," Alex said, refusing to take his hand.

Luke reached out and grabbed her hand despite her reluctance. He turned it palm up, studied it, then gently stroked the soft skin with slow, circular motions. He looked up at her.

"Yes, I am."

He said it softly, his voice as consuming a caress as the touch of his fingers on her hand. A man, yes, she thought, but one unlike any she knew. A compelling man. One who piqued her interest where no one before had even scratched the surface.

The quiet in the room was deafening. Alex pulled away from him and walked to the other side of the room. She needed space, but there was none. She turned to him and leaned her back against the door.

"Let's set some ground rules, Mr. Stratten."

"Luke."

"Luke, then. It appears we're going to be stuck here for some time. Maybe another day, maybe more. Whatever the case, I want you to know that what's been written about me is mostly false."

"Mostly?"

"Yes. The papers always have some small grain of truth in their stories. Something that justifies it. But the reality is that most everything else is fabricated."

"Do you want me to believe that you haven't had *thousands* of lovers?" he said with a grin.

Alex didn't return the teasing smile. "I don't care what you believe. I just want to be sure you understand that I am not 'fair game' while we are here in this situation."

Luke raised his eyebrows, but couldn't for the life of him wipe the grin off his face. "Am I to take that to mean that I shouldn't come on to you?"

Alex hesitated, then nodded. "Yes, I think that's the point I'm trying to make."

"Well, don't worry your pretty little head about that, sweetheart. I have less than no interest in making it with you." He amazed himself at how easily the lie came.

Alex felt her cheeks flame. Who did he think he was, speaking to her in that way? No matter. She wouldn't put herself on his level. "That's fine with me, Mr. Stratten."

"Luke," he said again.

"That's fine with me, *Luke,*" she repeated.

"Great," he said, and clapped his hands for control. What he really wanted to do was wipe that holier-than-thou expression off her face...with a kiss. "Now that we got that out of the way, what do you say we find something to eat around here?"

"Eat?" She couldn't believe he could think about food now.

"Yeah, I'm starving. You must be, too. When was the last time you had a meal?"

"Uh, I don't know. Yesterday morning?"

Luke rummaged through the cabinets. "Ta-dah!" He held up two cans of noodle soup. "A feast," he said with a broad grin.

God, he was handsome, Alex thought. Standing there like a jerk with two cans in his hands, she still couldn't help but admire his face and body. Why was that? She'd meant every last word she'd said to him. She didn't want any involvement—no matter how brief—with any man, especially now when she was ready to make a new commitment in her life. Yet she also couldn't deny that there was a part of her that was hugely attracted to him, despite, or perhaps because of, his total inappropriateness.

She thought of Justin Farrell and her not-to-be marriage. She had no remorse about calling off the wedding, yet there was a well deep inside her filled with sadness and longing for a life of fulfillment that seemed unattainable. No matter how many times she rationalized to the contrary, she did "want it all."

Luke opened the cans of soup and dumped the contents into another pot he found in the cabinet underneath the sink. Adding water, he swished it around and headed to the stove. He turned the knob, lit a match, and set the pot on top of the burner.

Soon the room was filled with the aroma of chicken soup. Alex's stomach began to growl, and she moved closer to the source of the tantalizing smell. Luke grinned at her over his shoulder as he completed his task. He set the pot down on the table and placed a spoon on her end.

"Dig in," he said.

Her mouth dropped open as she watched him eat out of the pot. "Aren't you going to serve the soup?"

"Serve it where?" he asked.

"In bowls."

"What for?"

"Because you're eating out of the pot."

"So?"

"Well, it's . . . it's . . . just not done."

He laughed out loud. " 'Not done'? You've got to be kidding. Take a look around, Alexandra. This isn't the Ritz, and I'm not your damned butler." He picked up the extra spoon and held it out to her. "Here. Help yourself before it's all gone."

She grabbed the spoon as he resumed eating. Though unbelievably annoyed with him, her stomach had no such problem. It growled. Loud. Luke looked up at her and grinned, his mouth full of soup and noodles. The cad, she thought, but nevertheless took a step forward and sat across from him.

Reluctantly she dipped her spoon into the soup and tasted it. It was good, so good her mouth began to water in earnest. She was starved, and until the moment the soup hit her mouth, she hadn't realized how much. Without any more prodding, she dug into the pot with a vengeance.

Their spoons clinked in battle over the last broken noodles. Luke stopped eating and set his spoon on the table. Alex stopped, too, to see what he was up to.

"Go ahead," he said. "Finish it."

"Are you sure?" she asked. "It wasn't very much."

"Yeah, I'm sure," he said.

She looked like a hungry little kid to him, just home from school and ready for that long-awaited snack. He watched her eat, drinking in his fill of her with his eyes as she tipped the pot to get the last of the noodles. When she was finished, she looked at him and grinned. Without thinking, he reached over to brush a stray piece of noodle from her mouth.

As his finger continued to graze her bottom lip, the grin on Alex's face slowly faded. She was mesmerized by his hot whiskey eyes and the scrape of his callused thumb. His touch lingered, long after whatever it was he was trying to clean away had disappeared. She didn't pull back; she couldn't. He held her with some sort of invisible ray, and she felt as trapped as an animal in the headlights of an oncoming truck.

Luke's not-so-full stomach rolled over at the sight of her smoky brown eyes at half mast. Good Lord, but she did things to him with that come-hither look that she didn't even realize she was giving—which made it so much more potent.

Wrong.

He dropped his hand away, pushed the chair out, and stood. Checking through the cabinets, he found a clean mug and brought it over to the table. He lifted the pot and poured the remaining cooled broth into the mug, then set it down in front of Alex with a thud. Some of the contents splashed out over the sides and onto the tabletop.

"Your soup, Your Highness," he said, and turned to walk away.

Maybe it was what he said, or maybe only *the way* he said it, but suddenly, and irrationally, Alex felt the blood rise to her face with such a vengeance that if she'd had a cork, she would have popped. Instead, she picked up the dripping mug and tossed its contents directly at him. It caught the right side of his head, chest and shoulder. Luke flinched as the broth hit him, then stood stone-still as the liquid seeped into the fabric of his plaid shirt and dripped off of the tips of his fingers.

Then he turned to face her.

The fury in his eyes was something to behold. It was powerful, threatening, heart-poundingly scary, and incredibly exciting. Alex pushed her chair out and stood slowly. She swayed toward him, as if a powerful tractor beam radiated from him ordering her forward. Gripping the table, she stood her ground, unaware that she had a choice about it. Luke pinned her with his eyes, and then with his hands as he grabbed hold of her shoulders and pulled her toward him with a teeth-rattling shake.

"What the hell was that for?" he roared.

His voice was deep and scratchy to begin with, but in high gear, it was stomach-clenchingly awesome.

Alex didn't answer him. She couldn't. She had no idea why she had done such a thing. It had taken her years to learn how to keep her volatile redhead's temper under wraps. The Alexandra Beck of today was not the impetuous teenage girl who had ranted and raved. This Alexandra was coolly elegant, and always very much in control.

It was totally unlike her not to think before she acted, yet she had impulsively responded to his mild gibe. The question was, why? She knew what he thought of her—it was the same thing everyone thought of her. Yet while it was all right for the others to do so, she didn't want *him* to classify her as useless, aimless and spoiled.

"Well?" he asked again.

She felt contrite, and wanted to say something that would make him understand why she had attacked him. Instead she lifted her hand to his cheek. With the softest, subtlest touch, she wiped the wetness from his face. The grip of his hands on her shoulders eased, massaged, then caressed. Her second hand joined the first, and she cupped his whiskered face in her hands.

"I'm sorry," she said in a very low voice.

Her words washed over him like a ripple of cool water. Luke began to tremble inside. She was driving him crazy. Cold. Hot. Cold. Hot. He couldn't stand much more of this, even if it was only going on in his own mind. But was it? Was he the only one feeling these feelings? Or was the little "hands off" speech just a ploy. Was she fighting a battle of her own?

He had to find out.

Luke pulled her against him. As their bodies touched, he stopped and looked down at her, giving her every opportunity in the world to pull away. She didn't. Slowly, with infinite care, he angled his head and brushed his mouth against hers. She was soft. She was warm. And her lips felt like heaven.

He deepened the kiss, and with it, shut his eyes to the world, entering a new one, more dangerous than any he'd ever traveled to on this earth. He parted her lips with his tongue, and she let him, opening her mouth in silent invitation to a most intimate invasion.

Luke wasted no time in accepting the invite. His tongue swept into her mouth, toying with her own, tasting her, eating her alive.

Alex heard a squeak, then realized it came from the back of her throat. She had never been kissed like this! His mouth totally conquered hers, and his tongue left no spot untouched. It was the most consuming, mind-boggling kiss she'd ever imagined. Her knees went weak, and she grabbed onto those broad shoulders for support. They didn't fail her, and she dug her fingers into the fabric of his shirt in silent gratitude for his strength.

Luke was lost. The world was spinning in his head, around and around and out of control. He pressed her body into his, and felt her melt against him, nurturing his hard arousal. If this was his battle to fight, defeat was imminent.

As she wrapped her arms around his neck and pulled him tighter, Luke felt her entangle her fingers in the longer hair at his nape. Was this the woman who had declared herself off limits? She sure had a funny way of showing it. Maybe it was all a game to her. She was used to playing games with men. Images of others standing in his place seeped into his mind and quickly cooled his ardor.

He broke the kiss. Her startled expression mirrored his own. Bodies locked together, they swayed but did not part. Luke blinked to recall reality, then lost it as his gaze centered on her slightly parted, pouting, swollen lips. He fought the urge to kiss her again... and again.

In desperation, he looked away and cradled her head against his chest. How many minutes ago had he lied about wanting her? The want was there big time, all raw and so basic, it scared the hell out of him.

He scanned the room, centering his gaze on the mattress and the blazing fire. It would be so easy to guide her over to that perfect setting. He would pull her down on the makeshift bed next to him. Slowly, he would lift her sweater over her head, caressing her skin as he revealed her full breasts to his view. He'd unhook her bra, and when he touched her, she would begin to shake with a need as powerful and urgent as his own....

She was shaking, all right, but as he drifted back to reality, he realized they were still standing by the table locked in an embrace. Her face was burrowed in his chest, and her shoulders were moving up and down. Was she crying? He leaned back to see.

No.

She was laughing.

"What's so funny?" Luke asked, his mood shattered.

Alex looked up at him. "You," she said. "You smell like chicken soup."

"And whose fault is that?"

"I said I was sorry," she said and pulled away from him, unprepared to comment on the effects of that kiss. "But you made me angry."

"I suppose it's my fault, then," he said.

"No, I take full responsibility. I shouldn't let what anyone thinks of me make a difference. Most times it doesn't, but this time . . ." She shrugged.

"This time?"

"It got to me. I guess I'm on edge. Why did you do that?"

She'd lost him. "Do what?"

"Kiss me. You said you had no interest in me."

"You looked like you wanted me to kiss you."

Alex shook her head. "I didn't."

"You did. And you kissed me back."

Alex bit her lip. He noticed that she did that a lot when she was thinking about something. He wished to hell she wouldn't, because every time she did, it set him off. Her lower lip was so full, so pouty, that she never quite managed to get it all in her mouth, and the sight of her perfect teeth biting into that plump little morsel was making him crazy.

Alex looked into his eyes. "I did . . . didn't I?" she said, more to herself than to him. "Take off your shirt."

"Excuse me?"

"Take off your shirt. I'll rinse it out in the sink."

Luke hesitated, then obeyed. Alex watched him unbutton each button with deliberate slowness. Was he trying to tempt her? The shirt hung open to reveal a tight gray T-shirt covering a very muscled chest. He undid the cuffs, shrugged out of the blue plaid flannel shirt, and held it out to her.

Alex stepped forward and took it from him without touching him. Turning, she held it to her as she walked toward the sink. As she turned on the tap, his scent assailed her. Traces of the chicken soup were obscured by his very personal man smell. It drifted over her like a slow-rolling fog, completely engulfing her senses as she soaked the fabric.

This was insane, crazy. Here she was, stuck in this nowhere place with a man she wasn't even sure she liked, and as unexpectedly as an apparition from heaven, she was feeling a feeling she had honestly never felt before.

Desire.

It had never been a familiar word in her vocabulary. She only used it infrequently, and usually to exaggerate something or other she wanted. She *desired* an outfit by the latest avant-garde designer. She *desired* a vacation in the south of France. She had a *fierce desire* for her father to butt out of her life... But she had never, ever, in all her years used that particular word in regard to a man.

Desiring a man conjured up all sorts of glorious possibilities. She knew all about them, but, contrary to public opinion, not firsthand. For sure, there were enough men out there to attest to the fact that they'd slept with her, but they'd lied.

When it had first happened, and she saw her former beau pontificating on a TV gossip show, she had been appalled. She'd even called the cad to complain. He'd laughed it off and called her a spoilsport. Who cared that she hadn't given it to him, everyone knew she'd given it to everyone else, didn't they? What difference did one more make? Anyway, he'd gotten paid for it.

After that, she'd become more protective. She would only date people she'd been introduced to, and then would only go to very public places with them. That didn't seem to help. When she'd refuse to go to bed with them, the same thing would happen over and over. Some asked what was wrong with them, some asked what was wrong with her, but most just got angry. Not one man had ever hung in there long enough to scratch below the surface of Alexandra Beck. All they saw was the long red hair, the shapely body, and lots of money.

It had turned her off completely at a young enough age that sex became something she'd decided to put on the back burner. As time went by, it became more sensible to abstain. After all, she'd reasoned, in the age of AIDS, it was probably the smart thing to do.

Trouble was, one year led into another, then another, until losing her virginity had become a monumental undertaking, one that required the most careful planning with the most perfect partner—a partner she never seemed to meet.

So, when all was said and done, Alexandra Beck was still a virgin. The Last American Virgin as far as she was concerned. The ironic part was that no one would ever believe her—and the only way to prove it was to lose it. That involved finding the one person worthy of knowing the truth. Problem was, there was no such man, and the older she became, the more choosy she became. At twenty-five, she firmly believed that the day might never come.

She lifted the dripping shirt from the sink and began to wring it out. Glancing over her shoulder, she noticed Luke sitting on the floor staring into the fire. Was he thinking about her and the kiss they'd shared? It had been powerful and all-consuming, and her reaction had probably helped to reinforce his opinion of her as a loose woman. Her heart sank with the thought. She didn't want him to think of her that way, and what was worse, she didn't know why.

"All done," she said, holding up the wet shirt for his inspection.

"Thanks," he said without turning.

Alex carried the shirt over to the fire. She pulled a chair closer and draped the shirt neatly across the back. "That's all you have to say? You didn't even look at it. See? Not one stain left."

Luke turned to her. He looked devilish sitting there on the floor in front of the fire with the reflection of the yellow flames dancing in his tawny eyes. Devilish, and absolutely, positively, the most gorgeous man she'd ever seen in her entire life. Or was he beginning to appeal to her more and more as time went on? Could a man grow on you? she wondered.

"The shirt looks very nice, Alexandra," he said with a smoky voice. "You are, without a doubt, a very talented lady."

For the briefest moment she felt threatened, not by the compliment itself, but by the way he said it. Besides, she wasn't altogether sure he was talking about her clothes-washing ability. No, not sure at all. What he may have meant would take a bit of thought, but the way he was looking at her right now was certainly not conducive to any coherent thought on her part.

Alex replied with a small smile before moving a safe distance from him. She walked over to the window. It was still snowing. She watched as one lonely flake drifted away from the rest and planted itself on the windowpane. There it stuck, frozen in a moment's time waiting for fate and the elements to release it from bondage.

She could relate to that little snowflake, only she wasn't so sure anymore where her prison truly was, inside this little cabin—or inside her head.

Five

Luke was brooding. He couldn't believe what he'd done. After all those self-inflicted words of wisdom about not going anywhere near her, he had not only touched, but kissed her. And, despite her denial, she had kissed him back. Thoroughly.

He stood and began to pace the small room.

"What's wrong?" Alex asked.

"Nothing."

"Why are you pacing?"

"I need to move," he said, then stopped.

For a long moment he stared at her. Seeming to make a decision, he walked toward the door. Alex watched him lift his jacket off the hook and put it on.

"Where are you going?" she asked.

"Out."

"Out where? It's still snowing very hard, and you have no shirt on. You'll get sick."

"That would be a godsend," he muttered.

"What did you say?"

"Nothing."

"Luke—"

He swung open the door and cold air blew into the cabin. "I'm going out," he said, and did.

The door slammed and Alex stood dumbfounded, staring at it. She shook her head as if to clear it, then walked over to the window. Peeking to the left and right, she couldn't find him. She was just about to turn away when he came into view.

He began to pace again, and seemed to be talking—no, arguing with someone. His arms were moving, and his hands gesturing. Alex looked around, but he was completely alone. Perhaps it was cabin fever. Perhaps he was losing his mind. She didn't know what was going on inside his head, but she was sure that it had something to do with her.

Something to do with that kiss.

She might be a virgin, but she was far from naive. She knew very well when a man was turned on, and Luke Stratten had been very turned on. That would be dangerous in many circumstances, and none more so than this one where they were virtually trapped and isolated. Alex had no doubt that if he wanted to have his way with her, so to speak, he would have no problem accomplishing it with ease.

Yet she had no fear. Oddly, the idea, once planted, quickly began to take root and grow. She really didn't want to get involved with a man, but there were degrees of involvement. He was, after all, a very attractive man. She was, after all, a very healthy young woman. Now that her career path was decided, one of

her short-term personal goals was to rid herself of this
burden of virginity as soon as possible.

Why not here?

Why not now?

Why not . . . with him?

He looked fit, although it was hard to tell that from
looks alone. She could ask him about his sexual history, she supposed, but he could lie. But then, so could
any man she might meet to perform the service.

Alex bit her lip as these myriad thoughts ran
through her head. Luke had stopped arguing with his
imaginary adversary. She watched him as he stared
into the thick snow-encrusted forest; the only visible
sign of life was his smoky breath. He stood still for the
longest time, like a statue. Alex waited for him to
move.

He did. As if he'd heard her siren's call, he turned
slowly, almost full circle. Through the fogged windowpane, their eyes met and held. Luke made no motion toward her. He didn't have to. The look in his eyes
was sending a powerful, invisible message. Alex's
heart began to pound, and her palms began to per-
spire as she responded.

He was almost completely covered with snow now,
and struck an ominous figure. She knew he must be
freezing, yet he still didn't move. A decision had to be
made, and instinctively, Alex knew it was up to her to
make it. Eyes never leaving his, she took one step back
from the window, then another, and another still, until she was too far away to clearly see his face.

Luke watched her as she faded from view, a dim
figure framed within the small oval of clear glass left
by condensation and drifting snow. She looked ethereal, achingly beautiful, as unreal as he felt . . . as if he

had entered some strange new world where reality was measured only in sensual terms.

Despite the cold chilling his body, his senses were on fire with a burning desire to touch her, taste her, see, hear and breathe her. He glanced at the sky. It was dark gray, with the storm showing no signs of letting up. Since they'd been literally thrown together, he had lost all sense of time and place.

He wanted her. That was the fact of the matter, and if nothing else, he was a man who dealt in facts, believed in them, lived by them. Pretending they didn't exist had never been one of his strong points, but never had it been more important to look the other way than it was now. There was more at stake here than a quick roll in the hay. He felt threatened by her in a very elemental way, as if she had the power to strip him raw, right down to his very bones.

He couldn't let that happen. He prided himself on his self-control, on his ability to keep things in their proper perspective. Why should it be so difficult to keep away from one wisp of a woman?

It shouldn't. And that was another fact. Luke filled his lungs with air and watched his smoky breath dissipate in the cold. He could do it. He could keep away from her for as long as he needed to do so. One little slip didn't mean he was beyond hope. A kiss is just a kiss, as the song goes, he told himself, and it had been the first and last.

His stomach growled, but he paid it no mind. As hungry as he was, there was no way he was going to share a meal with her again…at least, not right away. He turned and stomped in the direction of the protected woodpile in back of the cabin. They didn't need any more wood, but he might as well do something to work off this excess energy.

Alex listened intently behind the door. She heard his footsteps come closer, then become fainter as he made his way around the back of the cabin. She ran toward the spiral staircase and quickly climbed it to look out the back window from the bedroom above. Luke hovered over the woodpile, then hauled a stack away under his arms.

Again, he was muttering to himself, and she wondered whether or not he had come to any conclusions in his argument with himself. She ran downstairs just in time to hear him drop the logs outside the front door. She was just about to open the door for him when she heard him stomp away again.

This was too much! This back-and-forth pacing and stomping was giving her a major headache. Never a very patient person to begin with, Alex grabbed her fake fur jacket and put it on as she left the cabin. She found him leaning up against the stack of wood, lost once again in thought.

Luke looked up and saw her. "What are you doing out here? Go back inside. It's cold."

"You're the one without the shirt on. Come back in."

"I'll be in in a minute."

"What are you doing?" she asked.

"Getting wood."

"We don't need wood."

"We will later. Now go back."

"No."

Luke pushed off the woodpile and walked over to her. "You're a pest, you know that?"

"Why am I a pest? Because I won't listen to you?"

"Because you won't leave me alone."

"I haven't bothered you."

"Oh, you bother me, all right." Luke tapped his head. "Up here."

Alex smiled. "Really?"

He noticed the smile, and hesitated. "Yeah."

They stood, not more than two feet apart, staring at each other. Alex couldn't wipe the grin off her face, and Luke couldn't manage to respond in kind.

"Go inside, Alexandra." It was an order.

"No."

"Alex—"

"Did you ever think that maybe I need some space, too? Maybe I'm as 'bothered' as you?"

Luke turned from her and lifted a stack of logs in his arms. He walked past her without answering her question.

"Well?" she called after him.

"I don't want to talk about it," he said without turning.

Alex gritted her teeth. He was the most chillingly controlled man she had ever met. Not even her light banter could crack that shell he had around him. One thing she absolutely hated was someone who wouldn't fight back. She didn't know how to handle him, and it exasperated her. She watched him turn the corner to the front of the cabin, and she stomped her foot in frustration.

Ambling around, she grabbed a handful of pristine white snow from the top of the woodpile. Her mind on Luke, she made quick work of fashioning a very respectable snowball, then tossed it from hand to hand as she continued her attempt to decipher this complex man.

Luke returned to find her juggling the snowball. "Don't even think about it," he said.

Alex looked first at him, then down at the snowball. She grinned. "How about a good free-for-all snowball fight?"

"No," he said, and walked past her.

"It'll be great exercise," she added.

"No."

"Come on, don't be a spoilsport."

"Alex, go back inside."

He was impossible. She pouted and headed back toward the house. Over her shoulder, she watched him fill his arms with wood. Impulsively, Alex threw the snowball at him. It landed with a soft thud in the center of his back. Still, he didn't turn.

"I said, I don't want to play," he said as he lifted more wood in his arms.

Just as he turned, Alex threw another. It hit him on the arm.

He growled her name in warning. "Alexandra . . ."

Ignoring him, she made new snowballs and threw each of them at him in rapid succession. One landed on his leg, one on his hip and the last hit him square on the forehead.

That did it. Luke dropped the wood and dove for her. Alex shrieked and tried to run, but he was too fast. He tackled her and landed on top of her. She was laughing, but to Luke, there was nothing funny about the situation. It was a familiar scene, one he remembered well as her hips cradled his once again.

Alex stopped laughing once she caught a glimpse of the look on his face. She had never seen passion this raw this close up. She snuggled into him and felt the strength of his arousal against her. A sudden, sharp thrill shot through her, and with it came a sense of feminine power so heady she cast all her doubts to the March wind that blew around them. Like it or not, Luke Stratten, she said to herself, you are not as immune to me as you pretend.

The slow, utterly feline smile got him. He gave it up, and kissed her. It was a hard kiss, an almost angry kiss, as he ground his lips against hers.

Alex lifted her wet, cold hands to his face and placed her palms on his cheeks. He was warm, despite the snow, despite the wind, despite the fact that he had been outside a considerable time. The heat in him delighted her, and she parted her lips for him, making him groan into her mouth as his tongue found hers.

They touched, mated, and all was lost.

It was a long, luscious kiss, the kind that squeezes your stomach and curls your toes; the kind that dares you to close your eyes, and when you do, you get dizzy and out of breath; the kind of kiss that swallows the very air around you.

Luke was gone. His lips left hers as he nibbled his way across her face to the delicate line of her jaw and below, to that same soft spot at the base of her throat where he had felt for her pulse less than a day ago.

He froze. Not from the weather, but from the realization that in less than twenty-four hours, he had lost whatever semblance of self-control he'd ever had. Rising on his elbows, he looked down at her face. Her eyes were closed, perfect, dark brown, half-moon lashes framing her large eyes. She lifted her lips to him in silent invitation. He groaned inwardly, but pulled back ever so slightly in refusal.

Alex opened her eyes. "What's wrong?" she asked, her voice huskier than normal.

"This is." Yet even as he said it, his body sank a little heavier into hers.

"Why? We're both adults."

"And in one day, two at the most, we'll go our separate ways." He shut his eyes. She felt too good. "It's better if we remain strangers."

"What if I don't agree?" she asked. "What if I say I don't want to stay strangers?"

"Don't." It was a warning.

"Are you trying to make me afraid of you, Luke?"

"That would be wise, but no. I'm just trying to make you understand. I'm leaving the country as soon as we get back."

"And you think that I'll cling to you and plead for your undying love?"

"I didn't say—"

Alex pushed him off her and rolled away from him. In one fluid motion, she was on her feet looking down at him.

"Well, don't flatter yourself, Mr. Stratten. I've never had to *beg* a man to make love with me, and I certainly have no intention of starting with a poor excuse like you."

"A poor—"

Alexandra left him. Within seconds, he heard the front door of the cabin slam. Suddenly he was cold as could be, and wondered if she'd locked him out. It would serve him right if she did, he supposed. He wasn't handling her very well. Hell, he wasn't handling himself very well.

He groaned, out loud this time, a roar of frustration. Pushing himself up, he felt the stabbing pain in his knee. He'd landed hard on it when he tackled her. Great, just great, he said to himself as he limped toward the door of the cabin.

The snow was falling steadily, and it was approaching late afternoon. There was still only one bed in there, and he was still going to have to share it with her. The thought caused him another kind of pain, a dull throbbing ache in the one spot on his entire body that seemed to be *totally* in control.

Luke dusted off the excess snow from wherever he could reach before trying the door. He opened it a crack and peeked inside. Alex was standing at the fire warming her hands. She didn't turn when he entered, nor when he shook out his jacket and hung it back on the hook next to hers. She still didn't acknowledge his presence when he approached the fireplace.

"Excuse me," she said, stepping around him as she walked over to the efficiency kitchen area.

Alex soothed her temper as she proceeded to clean up from lunch, then aggressively rewiped the already clean countertop. She peeked over her shoulder as Luke made several trips back and forth with armfuls of wood. After several grunts and groans, she turned to see what was wrong. He was having a hard time accomplishing the simple chore, and it was plain to see why. His knee. He could barely bend it, and was trying his best to hide the fact.

It was true that he was the most exasperating man she had ever known, even more so than her father. It was also true that his words had cut her, deeper than she would have believed possible. She had never been rebuffed by a man, and the feeling was disorienting—especially since he just happened to be the first man at whom she'd ever thrown herself. But he was hurting, too, physically at least, and Alexandra's natural compassion couldn't stand to watch anyone in pain.

"Take your jeans off," she said authoritatively.

Luke spun around at her words. "What?"

"Come on. Don't be shy," she said. "It's obvious your knee is hurting. Let me see what can be done."

Luke dropped a log onto the pile. "Since when are you a doctor?"

"I'm not. But I've studied nursing."

"You . . ." Luke was about to make a sarcastic remark when the defensive lift of her chin stopped him cold. "Sure," he said. "Give me a minute."

Alex turned her back to him and filled a pot with water. As she placed it on the stove, Luke stripped the quilt from the mattress and disappeared into the bathroom. He returned moments later with the quilt wrapped modestly around his middle.

"Lay down so I can look at it," she said.

Luke obeyed, silently watching as she folded back the quilt just enough to expose his right knee.

"Lord! What happened here?" she asked as she examined the scarred, swollen joint.

"Accident down in Central America."

"What were you doing in Central America?" she asked.

"Research," he said, then quickly added, "A mine blew near my Jeep. The kneecap got busted up. Doctor said something like a light bulb shattering."

"You've had surgery?" she asked.

"Yeah. I've got enough screws in there to set off the metal detectors at the airport."

Alex shook her head as she gingerly tested the swollen area. "This isn't really healed. You should have a brace."

"I do."

"Where is it?"

"In New York."

Alex raised her eyebrows. "A good place for it."

"I thought so," he said defiantly.

She shook her head and stood. "Men."

Luke watched her pour the heated water into a bowl. "What's that supposed to mean?"

"Just what it sounds like."

"You think we're all stupid, macho jerks, don't you?" he asked.

"You said it, not me."

He was about to continue the discussion when Alex returned and knelt next to him. She dipped a dish towel into the water and placed it over his knee. He changed his mind as he felt the warmth seep in. Leaning his head back, he shut his eyes and enjoyed the pampering. He couldn't remember the last time someone fussed over him, particularly a beautiful woman. It was a good feeling . . . one that came dangerously close to contentment.

Alex stood. "We'll leave this on for a while, then I'll pack the knee in snow. First warm, then cold."

Luke opened his eyes. "Where'd you learn all this?"

Alexandra squared her shoulders and faced him down. "I studied nursing at a very prestigious school in upstate New York for about four months last year. It was something I had always wanted to do. My mother was a nurse before she met my father. She died when I was a little girl. It may seem childish, but I wanted to be like her. I intended to make a career out of it."

"And? What happened?"

"The paparazzi got wind of it, that's what happened."

"You mean, the press reported that you were going to nursing school?"

Alex laughed derisively. "No, that's not what I mean. What I mean is that some tabloid reporters splashed the most ridiculous story about me 'playing' at nursing—or more specifically, playing *around* with a doctor. They even ran a paste-up photograph with my head on someone else's body in a nurse's uniform in a clinch with some guy in a white coat. It was awful. They camped out by the school twenty-four hours a day trying to take my picture and get a story. The whole school was disrupted. When they wouldn't stop, I was asked to leave."

She spoke so matter-of-factly, but Luke couldn't help but notice the wringing hands and trembling lips. This was difficult for her to talk about, and the whole episode was obviously very painful. No wonder she was defensive.

He was suddenly overwhelmed with compassion for what it must be like to be Alexandra Beck. He hadn't given it much thought, not in all the hours they'd been together. He'd been too busy thinking about himself and his reaction to her. But now a new picture began to form, one of a lovely but lonely woman who couldn't escape from the shadow of an overbearing and flamboyant father.

That he could relate to big-time.

"It's a shame that happened," he said. "I think you would have made a damned good nurse, Alexandra."

He meant it, too. Whether it was the touch of her soft, healing hands or the warm compress, his knee was feeling better already.

Alex didn't realize how tense she was until his words washed over her. She had never told anyone how hurt she had been by that episode in her life. It had represented the end of a childhood dream, and somehow it was important that he not ridicule her, that he understand. She smiled, tentatively at first, then with a full-fledged grin. She knelt, redipped the cloth and reapplied it to his knee.

"Thank you," she said softly. "You're the first person to ever take me seriously."

"Rough, huh?"

"Yes. Very rough. I'd thought I was used to them following me around all the time."

"Them?"

"Reporters. Sometimes it was even fun. You know, especially when I was younger and club-hopping. Seeing your picture in the papers the next day is heady stuff at sixteen. But then it all backfired. The older I got, the more outrageous the lies became. It's completely out of control. I try to ignore it, but..." She shrugged.

"But?"

"But no one lets me. You have no idea how tenacious reporters can be."

"Not all reporters are vultures," he said, trying not to sound too defensive.

This might be a perfect lead-in to tell her the truth about himself... or at least, part of the truth. He wasn't quite sure she was ready to hear all of it. He wasn't quite sure he was ready to tell all of it, either.

Alex reapplied the cloth. "Maybe not. But they're all liars. They'll lie, cheat, sell their grandmothers to be the first one to get a story. Believe me, I know firsthand."

So much for coming clean, Luke thought. Instead he placed his hand over hers and stilled her actions. She had an animated, almost angelic glow on her face as she looked at him, as if helping him was giving her a special kind of inner joy. God, she was beautiful, so perfectly formed, his photographer's eye wanted to capture this moment, this look, on film forever more.

"It feels a lot better now."

She smiled shyly. "I'm glad."

Luke followed Alex with his eyes as she stood and dumped the bowl of water down the drain.

"I'll just go out and get some snow," she said, and headed for the door.

"Alex," Luke called.

"Yes?"

"Thank you."

"You're welcome."

"And lucky."

"Lucky?"

"Yeah. If I had to get stuck in a snowstorm, I can't think of anyone better to be stuck with," he said.

"Because I'm such a good nurse?" she asked coyly.

He grinned. "Among other things."

"Well, that works both ways. I guess I'm lucky, too."

As they stared at each other something passed between them, a silent acknowledgment that a new plateau had been reached, one of mutual respect, and perhaps just a bit more understanding on his part.

As Luke watched her open the door and disappear over the threshold, a wave of apprehension washed over him. He'd been this close to telling her the truth. That was not only stupid, it was dangerous. No matter what he was beginning to feel for her, it would be wrong to force her to deal with this while they were still stranded. Time enough when they got out of here. Time enough then for him to straighten all this out.

In a flash, he made up his mind. Joe would have a conniption, but there was no way he was going to sell those hot tub pictures. Luke glanced at his jacket on the hook beside the door. He could easily get up and throw the roll of film into the fire and be done with it, but something stopped him. The pictures themselves were so beautiful, they bordered on artistic. He wanted to keep them, if only to torture himself in the years to come.

All the more reason for not telling her now, he rationalized. The door opened and Alex walked in with a bowlful of snow. She smiled at him, and he felt his heart somersault in his chest. God, if she kept looking at him like that, he'd be a goner for sure.

She knelt down beside him and gently ran her hand up his ankle to his knee. A jolt of pleasure shot up his leg and centered in his groin. He felt the heat rise as his body reacted with alarming speed to the feel of her hands on him.

Who was he kidding? It was already too late.

It had been from that first look through the lens of his camera.

Six

Luke was sleeping.

Alex pulled the quilt up to his chest and stared down at his peaceful form. She had packed his knee in snow for about an hour, and the redness had all but disappeared. After he had dressed, she had slipped a pillow under his knee to raise the leg and help reduce the swelling. He had been the most amiable patient, not even objecting when she'd suggested a nap before dinner. If she hadn't known better, she could almost believe he had even enjoyed the attention she'd given him.

She certainly had. Caring for him made her feel more useful than she had in years. He needed her— whether he liked it or not—for the duration of time they'd be here, and that suited her just fine.

Alex reached out; her hand stilled midway. She wanted to touch his brow, but didn't dare. She wasn't sure she wouldn't be the one to benefit more than he. It was so unusual, but once she'd touched him, she couldn't seem to keep her hands from him. She wanted to pet him, caress his face, run her hands over his shoulders, feel their width and strength. And more.

She wanted to feel his hands on her.

Alex smiled to herself. Who would have thought it could happen like this? She'd dreamed, of course, about the man who would be The One, but never in her wildest dreams had a situation like this ever materialized.

Yet her mind was made up. Myriad thoughts swirled through her head as to how she was going to seduce him. She had no doubt he wanted her, but piercing that shell he'd erected around himself would be an awesome task. She was sure she could do it, but she wasn't sure she'd have enough time.

Alex glanced out the window. Twilight filtered in through the window, and still the snow fell. Good. Once she'd made her decision, she'd said a few heartfelt prayers that the storm would last the night at the very least. She needed that extra time to work on him, to try to convince him that making love with her was the right thing to do, that he didn't have to fear she would hang on to him when they inevitably parted ways.

How to convince him was the question. She bit her lip, and pondered her next course of action. How would she go about this if they weren't trapped in this cabin? What would she do if she had met him back in New York?

She'd probably invite him to dinner at her apartment. She was a pretty good cook, which surprised most people. Cooking relaxed her, and she was fa-

mous for her dinner parties where she made a ritual of
trying out new recipes on her friends. She'd become
pretty adept at concocting innovative dishes out of the
ordinary. Why not do the same here? She could cook
him a dinner, and let nature take its course here just as
easily as she could in her Fifth Avenue apartment,
couldn't she?

Quietly she tiptoed over to the kitchen area and
rummaged through the cabinets. There were two cans
of tuna, a can of baked beans, a jar of Spanish olives, and more soup. The lazy Susan held a good as-
sortment of spices. Best of all, she found a hidden
bottle of Chardonnay lying on its side in the cabinet
next to the unplugged refrigerator.

Alex carried the bottle to the door, opened it a
crack, and thrust it into a pile of snow. She peeked
over her shoulder to check on Luke, but he never
moved a muscle. Buoyed by her good fortune, she set
out to prepare her slightly less-than-gourmet seduc-
tion feast.

She played around with the tuna, cutting up the olives and tossing it all with some of the brine. A dash
of lemon pepper made all the difference, and a tiny
taste told her she'd discovered the beginnings of a new
dish to try out on her friends. She filled a bowl with
snow and placed the tuna plate inside it to chill. Once
that was finished, she emptied the beans in the smaller
pot while she mixed two cans of vegetable soup in the
larger, setting both aside for heating. She arranged two
place settings.

Alex lit a long taper and surveyed her handiwork.
If she were home, what would she do now? A long,
hot bubble bath probably, but that was not possible.
She felt grubby from spending her second day in the

same clothing, and a quick shower might be better than none at all.

After checking Luke, she took the candle and entered the bathroom where she stripped down and, remembering Luke's words of warning, took the fastest shower on record. She dried off as quickly as possible using one of the well-worn towels left behind by the owners. She was shaking from the cold and loathe to put back on the same clothes, but there was no choice. She quickly donned her turtleneck sweater and ski pants, sans underwear. The least she could do was wash out her lingerie, she thought, and hung her clean bra, panties and hose over the stall.

She did her best to check herself in the poor lighting. Her hair was damp and unruly. Since she had no brush, she ran her fingers through the long tresses and shook her head to restore its natural fullness. Her face was shiny clean, her complexion rosy. She bit her lips, producing a very attractive pink pout. She puckered and kissed the air. Not bad, she thought, under the circumstances. She grinned broadly. Her skin tingled from the shower, and from the excitement of what she was about to do. She felt a wonderful sense of naughtiness without any underwear, but then, if all went as planned, she wouldn't need it....

Luke was still asleep when she returned, and she took her time heating the soup and the beans. When they were almost ready, she retrieved the bottle of wine from outside and uncorked it. She poured herself a small amount and took a sip as she relaxed by the fire. Her stomach growled as the tantalizing aromas filled the small room.

Luke's did the same. But while the call of food roused him, it was an appetite of another kind that demanded equal time when he opened his eyes. Alex was sitting by the fire. The backlight produced an aura around her head. Her hair was damp around the edges, curling as it dried. She looked so damned beautiful, he felt his throat close up at the sight.

Awakening to such a sight reinforced the erotic dream he'd been having. He and Alex had been naked, their bodies locked together, rolling around on this very mattress in front of this very fire. The strength of his erection was mute testament to the stark reality of the dream.

As much as he knew he should shake himself out of this mood, he didn't have the energy to let it go. Instead he shifted and rolled over onto his side to get a better look at Alexandra.

Alex caught his movement. "You're up," she said.

You could say that again. "Yeah. What's that I smell?" he asked in a voice mellowed by sleep.

"Dinner?"

"Mmm...that, but something else, too. You."

"Me?"

"Yeah, you smell like flowers."

"I showered."

"Was the water hot enough?"

Alex shrugged. "Tepid, but better than nothing. I'm afraid I couldn't stand myself any longer."

Luke rubbed his two-day-old stubble. Maybe she had a point. "That's not a bad idea. Any soap left?"

She crinkled her nose at him. "Enough."

Luke laughed. "I get the hint." He moved to stand.

"Here, let me help you," she said, rushing to his side.

With one arm around his waist, she forced him to rest the weight from his bad leg onto her. Luke wrapped his arm around her and allowed himself the luxury of rubbing his palm across her back. As his hand roamed up and down, a message seeped into his brain. He almost lost his footing, and the pain in his knee had nothing to do with it. He looked down at her for confirmation, then blinked rapidly to clear whatever cobwebs of sleep remained.

No bra.

He knew for a fact she'd been wearing one earlier, so what happened to it? He checked again. Yep, clear as day, her erect nipples poked through the fabric of her sweater. To a normal person, in normal circumstances, it would be no big deal. It probably wasn't even all that noticeable. Problem was, he was beyond normal, he was in a perpetual state of arousal. That being the case, an insignificant incidental such as a braless Alex took on monumental importance.

Now *why* did she do that? Why did she take off her bra—he glanced down below her waist and audibly swallowed—and whatever else?

His libido was in overdrive, pumping his blood through his veins at an alarming rate. He itched, among other things, to rub his fingertips against those pouting buds...those same pouting buds that had bobbed up and down while she'd soaked in the hot tub.

The image froze him to the spot. He dropped his hand. "I can make it the rest of the way on my own," he said, and limped toward the bathroom.

Luke lit a candle, shut the door, and leaned against the sink. Staring at his reflection in the mirror, he shook off a chill. Yes, sir, a shower was definitely in order. Forget tepid. He needed cold. As he pulled open the beveled glass shower door, something fell across his arm. Upon further inspection he recognized Alex's underwear... the errant bra, panty hose, and the skimpiest pair of panties he had ever seen in his life.

He shut his eyes and groaned. Get a grip, man, he said to himself, and quickly dropped her unmentionables into the sink. He stripped and jumped into the shower. He turned the knob to the coldest setting. The water pelted him with tiny needles of ice as he quickly soaped up and rinsed down. It did wonders in diminishing his ardor, and for that he was thankful.

Luke stepped out of the stall and dried off as best he could. Taking a lead from Alexandra, he discarded his briefs and slipped into his jeans. With infinite care, he rearranged Alex's lingerie over the shower door. He threw his T-shirt and briefs into the sink, washed them out, and hung them next to her things. For the longest moment he stared at the items hanging over the stall. The intimacy of the scene overwhelmed him.

So much for the cold shower.

He rubbed his whiskered face. He'd give a lot for a shave. Pulling open the medicine cabinet, he surveyed its contents. The owners seemed to be nothing if not efficient. There were various packs of sample toiletries. He found a small tube of toothpaste and used his finger for a brush, then found a sample pack of disposable razors sitting on the second shelf right next to the aspirin. There was no shaving cream, but that didn't throw him. He'd shaved under much harsher conditions than this.

Luke was about to shut the cabinet door and get started when his peripheral vision caught hold of a small, square, purple box partially hidden on the top shelf. His heart tripped as he instinctively acknowledged what it was. As if in slow motion, Luke reached for it, confirming, at the same time, his most ardent hope . . . and his worst fear.

He stared at the box of condoms feeling certain that someone up above was testing him.

No, he pleaded, don't do this to me. If there was one thing that had kept him in line it had been the fact that he'd had no protection. He wouldn't do that to her, or himself. Eliminating that problem virtually threw open the door to so many endless possibilities that his body began to tighten with just the hint of what they might be.

He swallowed hard. There was only one thing to do. Get rid of it. But how? He couldn't very well throw the box in the trash; Alex would see it. He checked around the small bathroom. There was no window and no hiding place. Maybe it would be best if he just put the box back where it was. She hadn't noticed it before, there was no reason to think she would now. He turned the box upside down and backward and hid it in the top corner of the cabinet. Tomorrow morning, he would slip it into his pocket and throw it into the woods.

Smiling at his noble ingenuity, Luke shut the cabinet door and proceeded to soap up his face. A knock sounded as he began to shave.

"Are you all right in there?" Alex called.

"Fine. I'll be right out."

"Don't be long. Dinner's ready," she announced.

"Great," he said. "I'm starved."

Luke finished up and opened the bathroom door to find his flannel shirt—cleaned and dried—hanging on the knob. He shrugged into it, but didn't button it up. Slowly, he made his way back on his own. The knee wasn't hurting as much after Alex's expert care, but he knew better than to push. If he wanted to walk out of this place on his own, he was going to have to take it easy. He may be stubborn when it came to his own abilities, but he wasn't a fool.

Alex stood beside the table with an anxious look on her face. She held out the chair for him. With a speculative look, he accepted her offer and sat. In an instant, she brought over a small step stool and lifted his foot onto it.

"There," she said. "That should do it."

"Thanks," he said, confused yet flattered at all the attention she was giving him.

Alex smiled at his bewildered expression. "I'll get dinner."

Luke watched her hop around the room like a cornered jackrabbit. What was she up to? He didn't know, and for the moment, didn't care. He couldn't keep his eyes from her. Her presence filled him with a sense of awe and peace. At the same time, the very air around them seemed to crackle with anticipation that only intensified whenever she passed by.

As Alex served dinner, her full breasts swayed very close to his face. Luke forced his hands under the table, clenching them to prevent himself from reaching out and touching each tempting mound. He succeeded in holding himself still, training his eyes instead on the unrecognizable contents of the plate she placed on the center of the table.

"What is this?" he asked.

"Tuna à la Spanish Olives," she answered.

"Never heard of it."

"That's because I just made it up." She scooped up a forkful and held it out to him. "Try it."

Reluctantly, Luke opened his mouth. As he chewed slowly, his eyes widened. "No bad," he said. "Not bad at all."

Alex held out a glass goblet. "Now wash it down with this."

He took a sip. "Wine."

"Yes."

"Where'd you get it?"

"It was hiding in the cabinet. Good, isn't it?"

"Yeah," he said, taking the glass from her and downing the remainder in one gulp.

"You're supposed to sip wine," she admonished.

"I'll sip the next one," he said, holding out his glass to be refilled.

Alex shook her head, but refilled it nevertheless. She dished out the chilled tuna, then took her seat across from him. She finished her own glass of wine as she watched him wolf down the food.

"Aren't you eating?" he asked.

"In a minute. This is much more interesting."

"What's more interesting?"

"Watching you."

Luke's fork stopped midway to his mouth. "Stop that," he said.

"Stop what?" she asked innocently.

"You know exactly what. What you're doing."

"Staring at you?"

"Staring at me like *that*."

"How am I staring at you?" she asked.

"Like I'm dessert," he answered.

"Mmm, sounds delicious."

Luke pushed back from the table. "Alex..." The warning was clear in his voice. "Don't do this. I'm not made of stone."

She reached out and caressed the line of his jaw. "So I see." She tilted her head. "Did you shave for me?"

"Alexandra—"

"No, don't answer that," she said as she rose. "Let's have our next course."

She served the soup with the beans on the side. It wasn't a very exotic meal, but Luke was too hungry to care. They ate in silence, finishing every last morsel of food.

"I guess we were hungry," she said as she lifted the dirty dishes from the table.

"Here," Luke said as he tried to stand, "let me help."

"No." She pushed him back in his seat.

"It's only fair I clean up. After all, you cooked," Luke said.

"Next time," she said. "Tonight, I order you to relax."

"Order me?"

"Yes. Order you."

"Yes, ma'am," he said, and gave her a mock salute.

"Drink your wine," she said with a shake of her head.

Alex made quick work of washing the dishes. When she completed the task, she walked up behind Luke. He was sitting on the chair with his foot resting on the stool, the wineglass propped against his good knee. Alex began massaging the back of his neck, and he leaned into the strokes of her hand.

"God that feels good," he said.

"Your muscles are very tight," she said.

Didn't he know it. "Must be sleeping on that mattress. Or should I say, trying to sleep?"

"Did I keep you up last night?" she asked.

"You? Hell, no," he said with a sarcastic laugh. "You only kicked me six or seven times, that's all."

Alex spun around to face him. "I'm a notoriously restless sleeper."

"Tell me about it," he said with a grin.

"Tell me about *you.*"

Luke shrugged. "Not much to tell," he answered cautiously.

"No wife?"

"No."

"No girlfriend?"

"Uh-uh."

"No one special at all?"

"No one."

"Why is that?" she asked. "You're certainly a good-looking man. Why hasn't someone snapped you up a long time ago?"

"I don't want to be snapped." He finished his wine and placed the glass on the floor. "How about you? There must be a line of guys out there just waiting to put a ring on your finger."

"There are..."

"I hear a 'but' there."

Alex smiled. "A big 'but,'" she said. "Most don't want me. They want what they think they see."

"And that is?"

"Looks, body, money—"

"Let's not forget modesty."

She punched his arm playfully. "That, too."

He grabbed her fist in his hand and pulled her around to face him. One by one, he uncurled her fingers and silently studied her palm. Alex's heart began to beat faster at his touch. He was so warm, so vital, so very much a man, she felt at a definite disadvantage with him. Yet he intrigued her, challenged her, excited her. She pulled her hand away and caressed his now smooth face.

Luke tried not to move. If he did, he knew what he would do. He would pull her onto his lap and kiss her so thoroughly that both their heads would spin. And then where would they be?

On a course to nowhere.

"You are a very handsome man, Luke Stratten," she whispered. "And I find, despite all your outward faults—" she grinned "—there is no one else I'd choose to be with right now."

She leaned down and kissed him. It was a mere brush of one set of lips to another, but to Luke's mind, a match had just been struck to dry tinders, igniting a raging fire inside him. In response, he clenched his teeth, forcing himself not to return the kiss. It was the hardest thing he'd ever done in his life.

"Luke..." Alex said softly against his mouth, "kiss me."

"No."

"Why? Don't you want to?"

"Yes, I want to."

"Then—"

Luke grabbed her upper arms. "Don't start something you can't finish."

"Who said I won't finish what I start?"

"Stop teasing, Alexandra. It's not becoming."

"What if I'm not teasing?"

Luke stared into her eyes. She was serious.

"Are you offering what I think you're offering?"

Alex swallowed hard. "Yes."

"Are you sure?" he asked.

"Yes, I'm sure."

Luke muttered an expletive, pushed her back and rose from the chair. He walked over to the sink, favoring his bad leg. For the longest time, he stared at her.

"Why are you doing this?" he asked. "Just this morning you laid a set of rules on me, and now all bets are off."

"I—I changed my mind. I want you to make love with me. Is that so terrible?"

"Terrible? No, it's not terrible. It's…crazy. That's what it is. Outright insane."

"Why is it so crazy? We're both adults. We're stuck here. I find you attractive. You find me attractive. Who's to know? Who's to care?"

"I care," he said softly. "And maybe I'm not up to being just one more notch on your bedpost."

"Is that what you think?" Alex felt unexpected tears well up.

Luke saw them in her eyes, heard the catch in her voice, and they pierced the rock-solid wall around his heart the way nothing else could. Like a robot, he left the sanctuary of his corner of the room and walked toward her. He took her in his arms and held her close to him, cradling her as if she were the most precious object he'd ever held.

"Do you really think that?" she repeated, her voice muffled against his shirt.

Luke lifted her head away from his chest. Threading his fingers through her hair, he held her fast. "No. I don't know why I said it. Yes, I do. I said it to stop you from doing this."

"Don't stop me. Don't stop yourself."

"One of us has to think straight. After tomorrow, we may never see each other again."

"Then let's have tonight. Just this one night... Luke?"

Her plea washed over him with a tidal wave of emotion. He kissed her. He had no choice, not really, not since the moment he'd awakened to her sitting in front of the fire. She'd taken care in preparing him a wonderful meal in the most basic of settings. When all was said and done, it had been the sexiest scene he had ever witnessed ... and it had all been for him.

He felt his sex swell against her. She must have felt it, too, because she moved into him, cradling his arousal between her legs. He parted her lips with his tongue and she accepted him, playing a mating game with her own. She tasted so sweet, a mixture of wine and woman, only better than any he'd ever tasted before.

Luke reached under her sweater. He ran his hands up and down her back and sides as he kissed her deeper. Her skin was soft, smooth, as silky as it looked. Fulfilling his dream, he cupped her breasts, one in each hand, and gently massaged each glorious mound. She murmured into his mouth, and the sound reverberated through his body, releasing shards of pleasure so intense he could barely keep his balance.

Alex felt him shift his weight and broke away. "Your knee—"

He pulled her back, slanting his mouth across hers in an all-consuming kiss that obliterated any concern she might have about his ability to stand on his own two feet.

When he began to lift her sweater, Alex shooed his hands away. Reaching down, she pulled the turtleneck up over her head and tossed it away. Shaking her hair, she stood before him, naked from the waist up. Luke stared at her with an intensity that seared her skin.

As she awaited his first move, she realized how truly vulnerable she'd left herself. Having always taken her looks for granted, she had never felt this aware of her own body. But here, now, offering herself to a man—this man—for the first time was so frightening yet so exciting that her body began to pulse with long-suppressed, long-denied desire.

"Touch me," she whispered, unable to stand there a minute longer without his hands on her.

Luke was going out of his mind. The camera hadn't lied. The sight of her, close up, was incredible. If he did as she asked, if he touched her, there would be nothing, no one, to stop him from making her his. He had never been a coward, never been intimidated by anything or anyone in all of his adult life, but this one woman offering herself to him scared the holy hell out of him.

Alex was shaking with want, with need. She reached out and splayed a palm inside his shirt. His heart was beating double time as she caressed the soft curls on his chest.

"Luke..." She moved closer to him, separating the material of his shirt and rubbing the tips of her breasts against his chest. "Touch me..."

As if with a will of their own, his hands obeyed her commands, ignoring the stern warning message sent by his brain. Luke touched her, rubbing his thumbs against her tight nipples, then gently rolling each bud between his fingers, tugging on them until they were hard pebbles.

Alex's knees gave way, and he held her to him for a long moment before both of them virtually collapsed onto the mattress. Luke kissed her deeply, his tongue sweeping into the recesses of her mouth, staking a claim as old as time. His lips left hers to kiss her neck, her collarbone, and the soft space between her breasts.

And then Luke threw caution to the wind. He opened his mouth wide and took her pouting nipple inside, suckling her as he'd dreamed of doing. She melted in his mouth like candy, so sweet, so deliciously female, that his already tight body throbbed with a desperate need to bury himself inside her. Instead he moved to the other breast and feasted on her in the same slow, steady, relentless way.

Alex was caught in a powerful vortex of desire. *This* was what her friends had talked about. This was what she had waited for. This was *it*. She wrapped her arms around his neck, running her fingers through the long hair at his nape, massaging the tight muscles of his shoulders, soothing the hard muscles of his arms as the magic of his mouth reduced her to a mindless pool of want.

She pushed her hips into his, not realizing why or what she was doing, only the need to satisfy some dark, elusive craving for more.

Luke ran his hand down her side, stopping at the waistband of her ski pants. He tugged on the zipper and released the button. The pants fell open, and hesitantly, he reached inside to caress her belly. Her skin was soft, her body firm, and he allowed himself the luxury of taking his time to explore her.

Alex would have none of it. She rotated her hips in time to each caress, demanding that he move faster, lower, down to the one spot on her body that needed his touch more than any other.

When he did touch her, she called out his name, over and over. The ache in her voice corresponded to the ache in his body. She separated her legs and lifted her hips into his hand, and his fingers grew bolder. Luke touched her intimately, dipping into her once, twice, over and over until they both were wild and out of control. He kissed her, and his insides began to shake. She was so wet, so open and needy that he was sure he would not be able to hold himself back a moment longer.

Alex was lost, gone somewhere out of this world as she normally knew it. She moved against his fingers in a frenzy, climbing toward a brightness so intense its glow warmed her very soul. And then it burst upon her, showering her mind with slivers of light so achingly beautiful that tears filled her eyes.

Luke felt her response, cupped her tightly as each spasm shook her body. He broke their kiss and nestled his lips in that soft spot behind her ear, giving her space, giving her room to breathe. His heart was pounding, his body on fire, rock hard and so in need of release, he thought he might embarrass himself.

He held her tightly, gritting his teeth to regain control. She'd reached her climax, and that, he told himself, was enough, all that mattered. He thought about the roll of film in his pocket and how he was deceiving her. He also thought of how she was going to feel when she discovered—which she no doubt would—who he was.

No, this was right; this was just. Under the circumstances, it was the least he could do. If nothing else, she would have this small pleasure to remember, and perhaps, some day, she would think kindly of him, even forgive him. And his punishment would be denying himself the one thing he found he wanted more than anything he'd ever wanted in his life. So be it; he would live.

Tonight was his gift to her.

Seven

Alex slipped into her sweater and lay back on the mattress. Luke rested on his elbow beside her. She curled into him, reaching out and gently scratching his chest hairs with the tips of her nails.

She smiled up at him. He didn't smile back. As a matter of fact, he was looking quite forlorn. He had made love *to* her, not *with* her. She felt contented, satiated, yet incomplete. She'd wanted to reciprocate, to please him as much as he'd pleased her. As she'd tried to oblige, he'd stopped her cold.

"Luke?"

"Hmm . . . ?"

"Why did you stop?"

He didn't answer.

"Don't you want to make love with me?"

"I want to. Very much."

"Then why didn't you . . . finish?"

He brushed a stray lock of red hair away from her forehead. "Because there are other things to consider."

"Like?"

"Like protection. I don't have any."

Alex shifted. "I hadn't given it a thought," she said.

But he obviously had. She wondered what he really thought about the kind of life she led. Yet, what good would it do to explain herself? Her old dilemma weighed her down like a ton of bricks. He wouldn't believe anything she said, anyway.

Alex turned away. Luke reached out and cupped her chin, bringing her back around to face him.

"You could get pregnant," he said.

His tawny eyes held hers. "Pregnant?" she said.

Maybe it was the wistful, little-girl quality to her voice, but her words conjured up a beautiful picture in his mind, one of Alex, cuddled against him just like this, with a baby—their baby—suckling at her very full, very beautiful breasts. A bittersweet pain twisted in his gut at the impossible thought, and he pushed it away.

Her eyelashes fluttered down, obscuring his view of her eyes. "I guess that would be inconvenient."

"Yeah. I guess it would."

She edged away from him. The distance was minute, but significant.

Alex's laugh had a tinny, artificial sound. "It's a good thing that one of us is thinking. If it were left up to me, we'd probably be rolling around the floor, making mad, passionate, mindless love all—"

"Alex. Stop it. I didn't mean to insult you. I wanted to make you happy. I thought I did."

She reached out and caressed his cheek. "Oh, Luke, you did, you did. It's just that I want to do the same for you."

Luke placed his hand over hers and shut his eyes. His body was still on fire, and he was still tight, hard and highly aroused from being near her, from hearing the melody of her voice, from breathing in her scent, which permeated his very skin.

"I don't want to do anything that will hurt you, Alex."

She smiled, a slow, very feminine smile. "I can't imagine your doing anything like that."

"You feel that way now, but once we're out of here, you may change your mind."

Once you find out who I am and what I've done.

"I won't," she said, conviction in her voice.

Luke stood. He had to. If he kept listening to her flawed logic, they'd be back in each other's arms, kissing, touching, and who knows what else. He had to be the one to keep things in their proper perspective. He was the one who knew the whole story. She was the innocent one. If he took advantage of this situation, she would never forgive him, and he wouldn't blame her.

When they were back in the real world, he'd tell her the truth, tell her that he had no intentions of selling the photos, tell her he wanted her for more than a one-night stand in a cold, isolated cabin in the woods. Then she'd be free to decide if that was what she wanted from someone like him . . . a reporter, the exact kind of someone she had come to despise.

He walked over to the table, reached for the bottle of wine, and refilled his glass.

"Me, too," she called out to him.

Luke filled her glass and carried it to her. Her hair was in disarray, a splendid mess of honey red silk. She flipped it over her shoulder as she reached for the glass. He had to physically stop himself from plunging his fingers into the silken strands.

"Thanks," she said, and lifted the glass to toast him.

They clinked glasses. "To avalanches and fate," he said, more to himself than to her.

"Fate?"

"What would you call our being stranded here together?"

She grinned. "Fate is fine. I'm just surprised to hear you say it. You don't seem the metaphysical type."

"There are depths to me of which you've yet to learn, dear heart," he said as he mock bowed before her.

Alex laughed. There was so much about him she wanted to know, but right now her ego was bruised and one question seemed more important than all the rest.

"Luke?"

"Yes."

"If we... well... I don't know how to put this without seeming silly."

"Just say it," he said, and sipped his wine.

"Okay. I will. If we *did* have protection, would you...?"

Luke's heart slammed in his chest. He swallowed the mouthful of wine. "Would I make love with you?"

"Yes. Would you?"

A picture of the small purple sample box of condoms hidden on the top shelf of the medicine cabinet flashed through Luke's mind. His right hand curled into a fist. He stared at her for the longest moment, his heart on his sleeve, and a look of longing in his eyes he wouldn't recognize even if he could see it.

"In a minute, sweetheart," he whispered. "In a New York minute."

A slow smile graced Alex's lips. She lifted the wineglass, and studied him over the rim. "Thank you," she said softly. "I guess I needed to hear that."

"You're welcome," he answered, secure in the knowledge that if the Lord above was giving out bonus points for little white lies and ironclad self-control, he had just niched out a golden throne in heaven.

She patted the spot next to her on the mattress, and against his better judgment, Luke joined her, reclining on one arm.

"I'm going to hold you to that, you know," she said.

"Hold me to what?"

"Your promise to make love with me. When we get out of here."

"You've got a deal," he said, "if that's what you still want."

Alex sat up. "What would change my mind?"

Luke shrugged. "Any number of things."

"Such as?"

"Once you're back with Daddy, things could change."

"I don't think you have to worry about that. Daddy's none too happy with me now. The wedding and all."

"Wedding?" He was getting really good at this.

Alex laughed. "That's what I like about you, Stratten. You're so well informed." She leaned closer to him. "*My* wedding. The one I ran away from."

"Who's the guy?" Luke asked as noncommittally as possible.

"His name is Justin Farrell, and he's a business associate of my father's. Almost his age, too. They both wanted this very badly." Her shoulders shook as if she'd caught a chill. "But I couldn't go through with it."

"Why not?"

"A lot of reasons."

"Then why did you agree to marry him?"

Alex shrugged. "Daddy caught me right after the mess with the nursing school. I was so confused, I didn't know what I wanted. Justin was sweet, kind and very patient. It seemed like a good idea at the time, but..."

"Go on."

"But I guess in the end it all came down to one thing. I didn't love him."

"Is that so important?"

"To me it is."

"Another hopeless romantic," he said.

"You say that like you know a lot of them."

"Maybe I do."

"Name one."

"My mother," he said, finishing his wine and placing the glass on the floor. "She was always searching for Prince Charming."

"I suppose that means she never found him."

"No, she didn't, but not for lack of trying. She was married five times before she died."

"So because of her failures, you've decided that being romantic is a major character flaw?"

"I didn't say that. I guess it's acceptable...in a woman."

Alex could feel her blood begin to perk. "But not in a man?"

"No."

"And why is that?"

"Because men live in the real world. Romance doesn't make the world go around. Money does. You should know that better than anyone."

"You sound like a real authority on the subject."

"Maybe I am," he said quietly.

Alex tilted her head toward him. She wanted to take him on about his comments about women, but something in his voice stopped her. Her desire to know more about him outweighed all else. "Tell me more," she said.

"Not much to tell. Suffice it to say that you're not the only one with an obsessive father."

"Yours, too? What does he do?"

"Banker."

"Are you close?"

Luke shook his head. "I haven't seen or heard from him in years. Let's just say we had a different view of life and went our separate ways."

"That's very sad. I feel sorry for both of you."

"Don't," Luke said, "it happened a long time ago."

"I guess that just proves my point."

"And that is?"

"Money doesn't make you happy. If it did, you and your father would still be in contact, and I would have everything I wanted."

"You don't?" Luke asked, truly curious.

Alex rose from the mattress and headed toward the table. She refilled her wineglass with the last drops from the bottle as she thought of a suitable reply.

She turned to face him. "No. Nobody does. But I'm not unhappy. I have a wonderful life. And it's going to get even better once I start my foundation."

"What's this all about?"

"I'm taking all my money—all my inheritance, I should say—and forming a charitable foundation."

"For what charity?"

"Not any one in particular. I want to offer grants to organizations and individuals who will help others."

"Sounds very altruistic for someone so young."

"Don't make fun of me, Luke. I'm very serious about this."

Luke didn't look at her as he spoke. He crossed his leg and rubbed his knee. "I'm not ridiculing you. Believe me, I think it's a great idea. But it just proves *my* point. Without that money, you'd have no foundation, so in reality, money does make you happy."

"That's not true. It won't buy anything that matters in life."

He laughed derisively. "I'd like to hear that list."

"Husband. Home. Kids."

Luke looked up at her. Visions of white picket fences danced in his head. Their gazes locked. "In that order?"

"Preferably," she said as she finished her wine.

"If that's what you want, then I wish you success in all your endeavors, both business and personal."

They had been doing so well, and then the wall had once again slammed down. Hard. Alex laughed, a short, nervous laugh. "You make it sound like we'll never see each other after this."

"We probably won't."

She took a step closer to him. "Why do you say things like that?"

"Because they're true."

Luke's head began to pound. These kinds of conversations always did that to him. He didn't know if it was his aversion to talking about his family, or her adolescent dreams of perfect love. All he knew was that his head felt as if it were about to explode, and he needed to get out of here. Fast. He got up.

"I don't know about that," Alex continued. "I thought that after... well, maybe we could remain... friends."

"Do you really think that's possible?"

"Why not?"

"Think about it. Life-styles and all that. I'm sure some very valid reasons will come to you." Luke walked over to the door.

"Where are you going?"

"Outside."

"It's pitch dark, and cold—"

"Cold is just what I need."

As he reached for the door, Alex moved up behind him. He could feel the heat from her body against his back. He didn't turn to face her. Instead he lowered his head and rested it against the door.

"Why are you doing this to me?" he asked in a low, harsh whisper.

"I don't know," she said honestly. "I only know that I'm very attracted to you. That I want you to feel the same way about me. That I want you to... want me, too."

Luke felt anger and desire churn and mix inside him—anger at what could never be, desire that was as relentless as the continuous driving snow.

He spun around, his face a mask of torment. "*Your* wants... that's all that matters, isn't it? Are you so spoiled that all you can think about is what you want? Not what anybody else feels? Not what's right, or wrong?'' Luke reached for her hand and guided it down below his waist. He pressed her palm against his sex, forcing her to feel every hard inch of him. ''Satisfied? You win. I want you. Now, please, let me go.''

He released her and moved to open the door.

''Not yet.''

Luke shut his eyes and blew out a breath. ''Now what?''

Alex touched his shoulder with a feather-light tap. ''This,'' she said, wrapping her arms around his neck.

She kissed him, little nibbling kisses planted around his mouth, his cheeks, his chin, and around each side of his neck. She feasted on him, even as he held stone-still, even as he refused to participate, she continued her assault.

She didn't know what she was doing or why she was doing it. Maybe he was right, maybe she was so spoiled that she didn't know how to take no for an answer. Maybe it was more than that. Maybe it was a combination of his words, the amount of wine she'd drunk, and all those lost and lonely years she'd spent dreaming about a man and a night like this.

Whatever the reason, all she knew was that she needed him, to hold her, touch her, make her feel like a woman as only he seemed able. Why was he making this so hard? Why couldn't he let her please him? He wanted her to, she'd proved that. Why was he fighting her?

She reached into his shirt, splaying her hands across his chest, feeling his heart beat double time as she caressed his flat male nipples with the pads of her thumbs.

Luke groaned. He couldn't resist her. She was already in his blood, dangerously close to seeping into his soul. He leaned over and kissed her. She opened her mouth and accepted his tongue. It was a bittersweet kiss that twisted his insides into knots. He'd never been as torn and tormented as this. In desperation, he pulled back from her, hot, achy, and out of breath.

"Don't be angry with me," she said.

"I'm not angry with you. I'm angry with myself for not being able to keep away from you. Don't you understand that?"

"Uh-uh," she answered.

"Stop that," he said.

"Stop what?"

"Stop looking at me with that look."

"What look is that?"

"Warm. Dreamy. Like you know something I don't."

"Is that how I look to you?" she asked.

"Yeah."

"Maybe it's the wine."

"Maybe."

"Then again," she said, "maybe not."

Alex reached up around his neck and pulled his head toward her. She slanted her lips across his and kissed him again, only this time, when his tongue touched hers, she melted against him, running her hands down his back, massaging his muscles as they flexed beneath her hands.

Luke wrapped his arms around her, spinning her around as all his good intentions vanished in a haze of desire so thick he couldn't see straight, let alone think. He tightened his grip, trapping her between him and the door. She shifted to accommodate him, and his rock-hard body nestled into hers.

He moved his lips across her cheek, down past her collarbone, to the space between her breasts, where he lingered, breathing in her scent. Driving himself wild with want and need, Luke mouthed her nipples through the material of her sweater.

Luke's hot, wet breath penetrated the fabric of her turtleneck, and soon she was writhing beneath his mouth, hungering for more of him . . . all of him. She reached and unsnapped the top of his jeans, insinuating her hand into the waistband. He gasped when she touched him.

Luke shut his eyes and held himself rigid as she wrapped her cool fingers around his hot length. His lips returned to hers, kissing her deeply, plunging his tongue into her mouth in tandem to the movements of her hand. He had to stop this, he knew that, but his body continued to move against her, demanding just one more second, maybe two, three . . . a minute.

He broke away from her, his breathing labored, his head pounding with a raging desire so intense there was only one way to accommodate it . . . and that way was forbidden.

"Alexandra, I can't take much more of this," he said.

"Then don't," she answered, her breathless plea fanning his neck.

Luke grabbed hold of her shoulders and pushed her back, holding her at arm's length. "I mean it," he said again, this time with more conviction.

"So do I."

"You're not going to win this," he said.

"I didn't know it was a contest."

"You've made it one. It's my will against yours, and I promise you, mine is stronger."

Alex took a step back from his grasp. "Don't be so sure. We aren't out of here yet."

"The storm's letting up," he said, "they'll come looking for us tomorrow."

"Let them. It won't change anything."

Luke shook his head. "Are you always so sure of yourself where men are concerned?"

Alexandra looked into his eyes. She knew what he wanted to know, but she didn't have the nerve to tell him the truth. Something deep inside her told her that if he knew she was a virgin, he'd run like hell. So, instead, she lied. "I've never failed before."

Luke felt a burning sensation somewhere in the vicinity of his heart, then chided himself. He had no right to feel this way about her. He had no right to even care. What kind of answer did he expect, anyway? She, unlike him, was only being honest.

"It's late," he said quietly. "Go on to bed."

Alex began to protest, but the look in his eyes changed her mind. "Where are you going?" she asked.

"Just outside. My head is pounding. I need some air."

Alex took a step toward him. "Luke—"

He held up his hand to cut her off, then rubbed his temple. "No more...not tonight."

Alex bit her lip, then nodded. She realized she couldn't push this any further. Perhaps his will was stronger than hers, but then again, she was tenacious. It was over, but only for now. Besides, he did look as if he were in pain.

She sighed. "Okay. Get some air, maybe it'll help. I'll get you a couple of aspirin." Alex turned from him and headed for the bathroom.

Luke exhaled a long-held breath, opened the door and stepped over the threshold. He shut the door behind him and breathed in the cold, crisp air. He flexed his knee several times, then looked up at the dark sky. The snow was still coming down, but the storm had reduced itself to a fine mist. By morning, he was sure, it would be over.

One more night, he told himself. Hold on for just one more night.

He rubbed his temples as he welcomed the night chill. It was helping to alleviate the pounding in his head. The aspirins would help even more.

His stomach flipped over.

He spun around toward the door.

Aspirins.

Medicine cabinet.

Alex....

Eight

_____

Alexandra glanced over her shoulder at Luke, who appeared out of nowhere. "Is something wrong?" she asked, her hand holding the medicine cabinet door open.

As he leaned casually against the bathroom doorjamb, his body radiated waves of cool, crisp night air in her direction.

"Uh-uh," he said. "What are you doing?"

"Aspirin, remember? I thought you were going to get some air?" she asked.

"You were right. It's too cold out," he said, and sidled up behind her. "My head feels better." He pushed the cabinet door shut with the palm of his hand. "Forget the aspirin."

"Luke, don't be silly," Alex said as she slapped his hand away and reopened the cabinet.

He slammed the door closed again. "No, really, I don't need them anymore."

Alexandra made a face. "What *is* wrong with you?"

As she pulled the door open again, his hand shot up to close it. Their elbows bumped and their hands collided into the shelves causing the entire contents of the cabinet to spill out onto and into the sink.

Alex and Luke stared at the various bottles, tubes...and the one small, but very visible, square purple box. Slowly, without a word or a touch of fanfare, their eyes met and held.

Alex lifted the box of condoms and stared at it for a long time. Luke watched as myriad emotions flashed across her face, culminating with a look of complete disillusionment.

"You knew about this, didn't you?" she asked.

There was no point in lying. "Yes."

Alex nodded her head slowly, recalling his earlier words. *In a minute, sweetheart. In a New York minute.* She felt her throat constrict.

"Excuse me," she said, and pushed past him as she exited the bathroom.

"Alexandra..." Luke called, then followed her out into the main room.

Her eyes caught the reflection of the fire and flashed as she looked at him. She began to pace back and forth as she alternately stared at the box in her hand and the man a few feet away.

"Why?" she asked.

"Why what?"

"Why did you put me through that ridiculously embarrassing conversation about making love and having protection when all the time you knew about *this?*'' She held up the box.

Luke took a step toward her, but didn't take the box. "I have my reasons."

"Oh, really? Would you like to share them with me? Would you like to tell me what kicks you got out of making a fool out of me?"

"You're not a foo—"

"Argh!" She shouted in frustration and threw the box into the fire.

Instinctively, Luke jumped forward, unthinkingly jamming his hand into the fireplace to retrieve the box.

"What the hell did you do that for?" he asked as he smothered the flaming box and threw it on the table.

"Why not?" she said. "We certainly have no use for them!"

She spun away from him. Grabbing her jacket off the hook, she pulled open the door.

"Where are you going?"

"Out."

"That's not going to solve anything."

"It works for you, doesn't it? Every time you can't stand being around me, you run outside."

He came up behind her and pushed the door shut. "It doesn't work," he said softly. His other arm came up to effectively trap her between him and the door. He leaned his body into her. "I can't run away from you. You're in my head—"

"Lies—"

"No. You're in my heart."

Alex shook her head, refusing to turn and look at him. She was angry, embarrassed, and so deep down hurt, she felt as if she had a knife lodged in her chest.

"Don't say things you don't mean just to make me feel better." Her voice reflected the strain of held-back tears.

Luke extricated the jacket from her fist and dropped it on the floor. He put his hands on her shoulders and turned her to face him. "I meant everything I said to you."

Tears pooled in her eyes. "What about—?"

"Everything."

"Then why—?"

"I have my reasons."

"You said that already. What reasons?"

Luke tilted his head back and stared at the beamed ceiling for a long moment before bringing his gaze back to Alex. "I'm not what you think I am."

"I don't know what that means," she said.

"It means that if you knew who I was you wouldn't want to... Let's just say, you'd run like hell."

"Who are you? A murderer?"

"No, don't be ridiculous," he said.

"A thief?"

"Alex—"

"Then what? What can you possibly be that's so terrible that you would think I wouldn't want you?"

"A reporter." Alexandra's mouth gaped open with his statement. A wry grin creased his face. "Close your mouth, Alex."

Her astonishment gave way to realization. "Then you *were* following me, weren't you?"

"Yes."

"I knew it!" She pushed away from him, pivoted, then turned back. "God," she said, almost to herself, "when am I going to learn to trust my first instincts? I *knew* you were after me. Who are you working for?"

He named a famous, albeit notorious tabloid.

Alex shook her head. "The absolute worst of the bunch. How *could* you?"

"I needed the money for my next trip."

"Africa, isn't it?" she asked.

"Yes. Africa."

Alex pointed to his bad knee. "And Central America?"

"That, too. I'm an investigative reporter."

"Then why are you working for that sleazy tabloid?" she asked.

Luke ran a hand through his hair. "I free-lance. Newsmagazines buy my stories, but they don't pay my way."

Alexandra pulled her hair back from her face. She twisted it into a knot on top of her head, and held it there. "Did you ever intend to tell me? Or was I just supposed to read all about it in the column next to the two-headed alien baby?"

"I intended to tell you when we got out of here. And there isn't going to be any story. I'm not selling it."

"Why? I'm sure it's worth a fortune. I can see the headline now—" she untwirled her hair and held up her hands in a freeze-frame "—I Romped Naked In the Snow With Alexandra Beck. It will probably finance two or more of your little 'trips.'"

"You know why."

"No," she said. "I don't know."

"Because what's happening here is no one's business. But ours."

The powerful stare from his tawny eyes penetrated through layers of hurt and pain. She wanted to hate him. She wanted to rant, rave, scratch his eyes out. She wanted to punch his chest, kick his *bad* knee, and grab hold of that fabulous long hair at his nape and yank hard. She wouldn't do any of those things, of course.

"I don't believe you," she said quietly.

"It's true. I didn't want to get into it while we were trapped here because..."

"Because...?"

"Because I didn't want to have this...discussion."

"Oh, is that what we're having? A discussion?" she asked.

"Alexandra, I'm trying to tell you the truth."

Alex studied him for a long time. "Is that all of it?"

Luke hesitated. He didn't have to tell her about the photographs, and she'd sure as hell never find out. He'd already made up his mind he wasn't going to sell them. As far as he was concerned, they didn't exist.

"Yes, that's all of it."

He stood perfectly still and held eye contact with her as she sized him up. It was, he felt, the least he could do. But after a while, his knee began to ache, and he got antsy.

"Say something," he said.

"What do you want me to say?"

"I don't know. Yell. Scream. Stamp your feet. Something. Anything. Just don't stand there staring at me."

"You hurt me, Luke Stratten," she said.

"I know."

"That's all you have to say?"

"I'm sorry?"

"Not good enough," she said. "I've thrown myself at you, and you've rejected me. I feel like such a..." She shut her eyes tightly for a moment before continuing. "If you didn't want me, you should have just said so."

"I do want you," he said softly.

"How much?"

"Very much."

Alex stared at him. She lifted her hand and pointed to the box of condoms on the table. "There's no excuse anymore," she said.

"No. There's no excuse."

She bit her lip. "Then...prove it."

Luke not only felt but heard the blood race to his head like an erupting geyser. He didn't answer her. He couldn't speak. He could barely breathe. His pulse was roaring in his ears, blotting out all coherent and rational thought. He took a step toward her.

"Don't just say it to be smart, Alex. Mean it."

She lifted her chin. "I mean it."

Luke took another step, then another still. Alex followed his progress with her eyes. As the portent of his intent hit her, her bravado failed her and she instinctively took one step back with each of his advancing steps. She stopped when her back met the kitchen counter and splayed her palms behind her for support.

And then he was standing in front of her, their bodies almost but not quite touching. Luke placed a hand on each side of her and hovered over her.

He's a very big man.

Where have you been, Alexandra? He hasn't *grown* in the past two minutes. But he did seem larger than before, towering over her in such a way that she had to tilt her head back to see his face. He wasn't exactly menacing, but he was...powerful. She felt her pulse quicken.

"Change your mind?"

"No."

"Good."

He slanted his mouth across hers and kissed her. Alex shut her eyes and let him lead the way. She reached up and held onto his strong shoulders for support. It was a good thing she did. This was a kiss with a capital *K*. He offered no sweet preliminaries, no little nibbles, no slow, sensuous brushing of one set of lips to another. His tongue invaded her mouth the moment his lips touched hers and swept through it with the force of an all-consuming hurricane.

Alex's lashes fluttered open. He was watching her as he kissed her. His whiskey eyes held hers straight and steady while his mouth made her dizzy. He seemed to be asking all sorts of questions, of her, of himself. She rose to her tiptoes and wrapped her leg around his ankle, pushing herself into him, rubbing herself against him, closer, closer, answering him loud and clear with her body language.

Luke's hands reached down and cupped her bottom. At first he tried to still her erotic movements, but as he felt her soft flesh in his hands, he began kneading and massaging her buttocks, fitting her into his hard arousal. A squeak emerged from the back of her throat as her body responded by melting down.

He lifted her onto the counter and positioned himself between her widespread knees. His lips left her mouth, to kiss her cheeks, her chin, the warm, soft spot behind her ear. Alex was breathing heavily, as if she'd just run a marathon. She couldn't keep her hands still, and they roamed over his chest, shoulders, back, as low as she could reach.

Luke pulled her sweater up only far enough to expose her breasts. He buried his face between the glorious mounds. Breathing in her scent, he tried his best to control his raging desire. It was no use. He had to taste her, take her into his mouth and suckle those sweet buds until they were as tight, full, pouting and hot as they had been the first time he'd seen them through the eye of his camera.

Alex threw her head back as he feasted on her. She ran her fingers through his hair, grasping handfuls and tugging hard with each corresponding pull of his mouth. She leaned down and kissed the top of his head, insinuating her hands into the collar of his shirt and caressing the hard muscles of his back. He was on fire, and the heat of his skin seared her.

His lips returned to hers, hungry and mindlessly searching to connect with her mouth. He cupped one breast in each hand, weighing the fullness in his palms as his thumbs flicked across her aching nipples. Alex's toes curled, and she clenched her thighs around him, crisscrossing her legs at his waist and locking her ankles together to hold him to her as tightly as possible.

Luke had no thought of escape. The only coherent thought he did have was to rid them of the barrier of clothing that seemed abrasive and coarse to his overly sensitive skin.

"I want to be here—" he pressed himself into her "—inside you. Oh, sweetheart, deep inside you."

"Yes," she whispered against his mouth. "Please. Oh, please, Luke. Now."

It was all the coaxing Luke needed. His tongue swept into her mouth as he lifted her off the counter and carried her to the mattress. Alex mumbled something as they passed the table, and Luke, without breaking stride, dipped her down. She let go of his shoulder only long enough to scoop the small purple box off the tabletop.

They fell together hard onto the mattress.

"Your knee—"

"What knee?"

The last thing on Luke's mind was his knee. There was only one part of his anatomy hurting right now, and at this particular moment, it was the only part in which he had any interest.

He kissed her as he fumbled with the waistband of her ski pants. Alex used the heel of one foot to push off first one boot, then the other. They worked together in a frenzy to disrobe her, and when they were through, all Luke could do was sit back and admire the perfection beneath.

"So beautiful..."

He ran one hand down her body, starting at the dip in her collarbone and moving slowly, caressingly, down her torso until he reached just above the one spot that was desperate for his touch. Alex was oblivious to her actions. She squirmed under the assault, separating her legs, lifting her hips ever so slightly to encourage him.

"Keep going, don't stop. Oh, Luke, touch me...all of me."

Luke obliged. He threaded his fingers through the nest of reddish curls. As he touched her intimately with the pad of his thumb, his entire body shuddered. She was so soft, and warm—and, as he continued his exploration—so very wet with desire. And it was all for him.

I give up.

He stood, pulled off his boots, and ripped his clothes off his body with such speed he had no thought or care as to where they landed.

Alex watched his acrobatic striptease, and her heart began to hammer in her chest. She had seen naked men before; her life-style had left little to the imagination. But nothing in her wildest dreams or experiences could have prepared her for the rush that pulsed through her body at the sight of Luke naked, proud, and thoroughly aroused.

She lifted her arms out to him and smiled. The very slow, seductive smile was his undoing. He lowered himself on top of her, gently settling himself between her legs as he bore the brunt of his weight on his elbows.

Luke kissed her neck, inhaling her distinctive, erotic woman's perfume. He was intoxicated and so lost to the world around him, he no longer knew or cared who she was, who he was, or what reasons had kept them apart.

Alex's body went limp under his. She was in a dreamlike state, responding to his every touch. And he touched every inch of her—with his fingers, his tongue, his lips, working his way down, nipping at her belly, her inner thighs. She knew he was marking her, but she didn't care. Not a bit. She smiled to herself. There was no one to see. Except him.

When he brought his lips back to hers, she was ready. She opened her mouth and initiated the kiss, touching her tongue to his, urging him to join them together. She was so ripe, so ready. All the years and all the doubts faded as she rejoiced in the luck, fate, or destiny that had brought him to her.

He was real.

He was right.

He was hers.

As Alex reached down and wrapped her fingers around his length, Luke groaned into her mouth, "Oh, sweetheart . . ."

He tried to pull back from her sensuous assault, wanting but failing to prolong the pleasure a moment more. He reached for the condom and quickly protected them. When he returned to her, he positioned himself just so, poised and ready to make them one.

"Now," she pleaded.

With one full, sure movement of his hips, Luke thrust into her. Almost, that was. Something was stopping him. His mind was too clouded with desire to think straight. He pulled back, and more purposefully, tried again. This time he felt Alex flinch beneath him. His mind might not be working properly, but his body responded immediately to her discomfort.

"Alex?" He looked down at her. Her eyes were filled with tears. "What's wrong?"

"Please, don't be mad," she said, her lashes sparkling with unshed tears.

"What . . . ?" he said as the realization of her virginity hit him like a heavyweight fist between the eyes. Luke's body was on fire . . . and in control of all his thoughts and actions. He shut his eyes and rested his forehead against hers. "Why didn't you tell me?"

"Would you have believed me?"

"No."

"You're going to stop, aren't you?" Her voice was ragged with fear.

Luke kissed her tears away, and shook his head. "No. Uh-uh. No way," he said. He threaded his fingers through her hair, holding her head in place as he gently brushed his lips against hers. "I don't want to hurt you, sweetheart, but there's no way on God's earth I will stop now. Not unless you want me to."

"I want *you*," she whispered. "All of you."

He felt himself swell inside her as her words caressed him. He'd meant what he said. He didn't want to cause her even the slightest pain, but cause it he must, if only for a moment.

"I'll make it up to you," he said, and with his promise, his body surged forward.

Alex dug her nails into his shoulders. The pain was there, but with it came a promise of pleasure so intense, she almost welcomed the initial discomfort. He stretched her, filled her, once and for all making her the woman she'd dreamed of being. He pulled out, almost entirely, then slowly, with the utmost care, slid back into her. He repeated the action, in, out, again, then again, until she lost all thought to sensation, instinctively moving with him, climbing, clinging, clawing toward a brightness that threatened to blind her.

He reached between their bodies and found the center of her desire. Slowly, steadily, surely, he stroked her with his thumb in tandem with their movements, and with his tender assault, he made good on his promise. Alex arched her back as the spasms began. A decadent, pagan moan began in the back of her throat and found its way out of her mouth. She bucked against him, simultaneously pushing and pulling at him as waves of pleasure grabbed hold of her and took her on the ride of her life.

Luke was no match for her uninhibited response. His body had been wound too tight for too long to fight her a minute longer. He gripped her buttocks in his hands, bringing her up high against him as he let himself go over the edge with her. It was the most glorious, powerful, soul-shattering climax he had ever had. He didn't even attempt to understand why that was. Instead he slowly rolled onto his side, connected to Alex in more ways than he'd like to admit, even now, at this most perfect moment in his life.

He drew back a strand of honey red hair from her face. She smiled at him and ran a finger across his full bottom lip.

"You are very vocal, Ms. Beck," Luke said, a half grin on his face.

"I *was* loud, wasn't I?"

"You'd wake the dead."

She playfully punched his shoulder, then rubbed the spot. "I didn't know it would be like that," she said softly.

"I know."

"Are you sorry?" she asked.

"For being the first to make love with you?"

"Yes."

"No. I just wish I had known. I would have tried to make it better."

"It couldn't have been any better." She brushed her lips against his. "Thank you, Luke Stratten."

"Oh, you're very, very welcome, Ms. Beck." He kissed her. This time with a warm, breath-mingling, reaffirming kiss. "Alex," he said, "do you have any idea what you do to me? I could take you again right now."

"Do it," she said.

He chuckled. "You'd be sore as hell if I did."

"I don't care."

Luke pulled away and stood. "Well, I do. I want you to be able to *walk* out of here."

Alex sat up and watched him step into his jeans, then make his way to the bathroom. "What's so great about walking?"

She heard him laugh, and smiled at herself. She was so utterly and completely happy, satisfied, and hungry for more all at the same time.

"Lay back," he said as he returned with a wet towel.

She obeyed as he gently washed away the evidence of their love. Each movement of his hand felt like a caress. Alex reached down and covered his hand with her own, moving with him as he attended to her.

"You know," she said, "I'm falling in love with you."

Luke's hand stilled for a moment before continuing. "Don't say things like that."

"Why not?"

"Because what you're feeling is only natural right now. Under the circumstances."

"Circumstances?"

"My being your first, and all. Kind of clouds the issue." He completed his task and moved back from her.

Alex stood. She picked up his discarded shirt and slipped into it. "And what is the issue?"

Luke stared at her, clad only in his unbuttoned shirt, which barely covered her creamy white thighs. He felt himself grow hard again, and marveled that he could react this way to her so soon. It seemed insane that he was so out of control, but she was like a drug, and without a doubt, he was already addicted.

"So? What is the issue?" Alex repeated.

"Come here," he said.

"What? Luke?"

He took hold of her hand and, as if in slow motion, pulled her to him. Luke pushed the shirt aside to cup her breasts. She swooned into him as he buried his face in her neck. Liquid warmth spread through her. She wanted him again, as much as he apparently wanted her.

"I thought you said if we made love again I wouldn't be able to walk out of here?"

Luke unzipped his jeans and guided her down onto the mattress. He brushed his lips against hers. "I'll carry you."

Nine

Alexandra refused to open her eyes. She didn't want it to be morning. She didn't want the light of day to insinuate reality into her dreamlike state. She didn't want the magic to end.

Please, not yet.

She snuggled down deeper into the cocoon of Luke's arms. They were locked, spoon-style, in the center of the old mattress. His long limbs were entwined with hers, his arms enfolded her as tenderly as a precious jewel. They were naked, warmed only by the patch quilt and the heat of their bodies.

Alexandra marveled that there could be any heat *left* in their bodies. It absolutely amazed her that they hadn't disintegrated, burned out, turn to ashes after the explosion of passion the night before.

Last night.

Had there ever been a night like that? Had two people ever touched each other on so many glorious levels before? Explored each other as thoroughly? Climbed an emotional mountain and found, actually *found* everything they had been looking for... and more?

They had been so in tune. Words were inadequate. Clichés about halves to a whole, two becoming one, were too trite and simplistic to describe what she'd experienced in Luke's arms.

She'd told him she was falling in love with him. That was a lie. She already was in love with him, probably had been from the moment she'd decided he was The One. In truth, she could have chosen anyone. The main reason she hadn't before was testament to the fact that she did not take such life-altering decisions lightly.

As worldly as she was, somewhere along the way she had picked up some very traditional values. Perhaps the fact that her father, despite his manic need for attention, had never remarried after her mother died. Alex knew that Felicia Beck had been the love of Victor's life. No one had ever seemed able to replace her in his heart.

His subtle message had obviously not been lost on Alexandra: when it's right, you'll know it. Tears squeezed out from beneath her lashes. She was exhilarated, beyond tired, and probably a little spacey. She was certain that was the reason for these out-of-control emotions.

She'd used the word love. Luke hadn't. That shield around his heart was so impenetrable it would take a blowtorch to pierce it. Once or twice during the night she felt she'd succeeded if only for a moment. That lingering gaze, softly spoken word and deep, soul-wrenching moan must have meant something. He couldn't have kissed her like that, touched her like that, tasted her like that and still remain unmoved, could he?

Alex remembered the look in his eyes just before they'd drifted off into exhausted sleep. It had been warm and tender. But loving?

All her lectures to the contrary, she wanted him to fall in love with her. She wouldn't kid herself. It was unimaginable that she would never see him again, that they would never share another night such as this. For all her bravado, she had not been looking for a one-night stand. She'd eliminated the burden of her virginity, but had taken on the worse burden of one-sided love.

She'd admit they had some very real differences, but they had some things in common, too. They'd both lost their mothers at impressionable ages, they both had domineering fathers, and they both didn't make commitments easily. She needed to convince Luke that they could make a life together. She wanted him, all of him, all the way. Could she do it?

Suffering from acute insecurity was a definite first for Alex. She decided that being in love wasn't what it was cracked up to be, especially when you jumped in feet first without looking. Her highly organized mind began to tick off her options. She had to sort things out, come up with a plan of action.

If she only had the time. But time had become her enemy. Slowly she opened her eyes, and her worst suspicions were confirmed.

It was morning.

And the sun was shining.

Time's up...

Alexandra stretched. She was sore in some very new and interesting places. She cherished every ache as each one represented a special memory from last night.

"Good morning."

Alex's heart swelled as she turned to face a smiling, tousled Luke. "*Great* morning," she said.

Luke laughed. "I'll take that as a compliment."

"Please do."

They stared at each other, their eyes reflecting the very vivid memories of what they'd shared.

Luke ran the pad of his thumb across her lower lip. "That was some night, Ms. Beck. I'll never forget it," he said.

She touched his cheek with the palm of her hand. "Nor will I. You definitely made it worth the wait, Mr. Stratten," she whispered.

Luke's heart slammed in his chest. Her words reached out and grabbed hold of him. Like a vise, they wouldn't let go. The night had been surreal, beginning with her offering herself to him. He had thought his gift of pleasure had been so selfless, so noble, but nothing could compare with the gift she had bestowed upon him.

And her virginity had been a gift, one he'd never presumed to receive from anyone, ever. It was true he had agonized over making love with her, but once she'd accepted the truth about who he was, all obstacles had, to his mind, been eliminated. He would have never guessed in a million years that he was to be her first lover.

The thought boggled the mind. Joe had spared no detail in listing Alexandra's exploits with men. To discover they had all been false, lies fabricated by the very press of whom he was part, turned him inside out. He didn't know what he thought anymore...or what he felt.

"We need to talk," he said.

"I agree," she answered.

"You should have told me you were a virgin."

"I told you last night. You wouldn't have believed me."

"You should have tried anyway."

"Why?"

"Because..."

She reached up and caressed the nape of his neck. "Why because...?

"Because it changes things."

Her heart skipped a beat. "Oh?"

"I feel..." Luke removed his arms from around her. He sat up. "I don't know how to say this."

Alex tensed. "I would think you could say anything to me after last night."

Luke blew out a breath. "Alex, listen to me. I don't want to hurt you."

"I may have been a virgin, Luke, but that doesn't make me fragile," she said, every aching muscle of her body on alert.

"It's just that I'm not the dependable type. Do you know what I mean?"

"You travel around a lot, is that it?"

He leaned back, a relieved smile on his face. "That's *exactly* it. I'm here. I'm there. I'm off and running at a minute's notice."

"And you think I will want to tie you down, is that it?"

"I didn't say that. Let me explain—"

Alex shimmied away from him as all her defenses rose to the surface with the force of an erupting volcano.

"You don't have to. I can see by the look in your eyes that you think I'll be some sort of panting female clinging to your leg as you try to get on the plane."

"That's not—"

Alex rose, totally oblivious to the fact that she was stark naked. "Yes, it is. Don't deny it. That's exactly what you think. Well, please don't feel obligated on my account. I'm a big girl, in case you haven't noticed."

"I noticed."

She spun away from his smug look, and, as regally as she could in her naked state, marched off toward the bathroom. When he didn't follow, she slammed the door and leaned against the sink, fighting the tears that were threatening to clog her throat.

Alex reached over and turned on the shower. Cold water splashed across her arm, but she barely felt it. Her frustration made her immune to such mundane feelings as hot and cold.

Damn him! How could he take the most beautiful night of her life and tear it to shreds with his callous remark? Worse, how could she let his words affect her like this? With the back of her hand, she dashed tears from her eyes, then turned the faucet to the hottest setting before stepping into the shower stall.

Droplets of warm water pelted her skin. She lifted her face into it, her tears mingling with the spray. As she reached for the soap, the stall door swung open. Luke stood before her with the quilt wrapped around him. Without a word, he dropped the blanket and stepped in behind her. He pulled her body up against his.

"Don't—" she began.

"No, *you* don't. To begin with, *don't* put words into my mouth."

The water streamed over them as Luke's hands roamed over her breasts and belly. Despite her annoyance with him, Alex couldn't stop herself from responding to his touch. The water began to cool, but neither of them noticed.

"I don't feel 'obligated,'" he continued. "I feel confused, mixed up, unsure, but definitely not obligated. All I was going to ask for was time for both of us to sort this out."

The water turned cold as she turned in his arms. "Do you mean that?"

Luke grabbed the soap and began rubbing it up and down her back and buttocks. "What do you think?" he asked as he pressed himself into her.

His sex was hard against her belly. "I thought cold showers were supposed to diminish a man's ardor," she said.

"I think that only works if you shower alone," he said.

Alex grabbed the soap from his hands and returned the favor. She gloried in running her fingers over his slick body. When she touched him intimately, he growled his approval. Slanting his lips across hers, Luke took her mouth in an all-consuming kiss. Alex met him halfway, her tongue gliding against his teeth in invitation to join her. He did, and the kiss deepened. Alex began to tremble in his arms, and he pulled back.

"Are you shaking from the cold or from me?" he asked.

"Both."

He fiddled with the faucets, but his actions only produced more cold water. "I think we're finally out of propane. Maybe we should continue this by the fire."

They quickly rinsed down. Luke jumped out of the stall first. He picked up the discarded quilt and pulled it around himself. He held it open, and Alex stepped into his embrace as he enfolded them both in the warm folds.

"Mmm," she said.

"Better?"

"Much."

"Come on."

They dried off by the fire while munching on peanut butter and crackers. Alex stared at Luke, drinking in each movement he made, imprinting the image on the negative of her mind. She had a sinking feeling that when all was said and done, it may be all she had left.

"Storm's over," Luke said.

"The sun's shining," Alex added.

"They'll be out looking for us today."

"I know."

"We probably should help out," he said.

"How?"

"Pump up the fire so they'll see the smoke. Try to get to the nearest trail. Follow that road to see where it leads. Hell, I don't know. We should do *something*."

"Yes, you're right, of course. We should do something," Alex said as she stood. She began to dress.

"What are you doing?" Luke asked.

"If we're going to trudge through the snow, I thought I'd better dress first."

Luke grinned. "I don't know. Ever since you mentioned that title for the article, I've been kind of fantasizing about you romping around naked in the snow."

"You're impossible," she said, holding her hand out to him. "Let's go, lazy bones."

Luke took hold of her proffered hand and got up. She had a point. He was becoming lazy. Lazy and content. For someone who could never sit still for very long, he was suddenly quite content to lounge around this tiny cabin all day. It made him wonder what he had been running to—or from—all the time. Every moment of his adult life had been filled with some nameless urgency. He'd called it adventure. Now he wondered if that was true.

He was beginning to question a lot of things. That unsettling feeling reestablished itself in the center of his gut. White picket fences seemed to loom large on the horizon of his mind. He dismissed them. Enjoy the fantasy, Stratten, he told himself. Don't blow the first good thing that has ever happened to you by getting in a mood about it.

While Luke dressed, Alex peeked out front. A ray of glorious sunshine fell across her face, and she tilted her head back to luxuriate in it. The wind had died down. There was still a chill in the air, but all in all, the weather was mild. Heavy globs of snow hung precariously from the bushes and trees, melting into rivulets of water.

She grabbed Luke's jacket, which was readily available on the hook near the door, and threw it over her shoulders. Leaving the door ajar, she stepped outside.

"Hey," Luke called out, "wait for me."

"I will." She took a deep breath of fresh air. "It's wonderful out here!"

A breeze caught her and she snaked her arms into Luke's jacket for warmth. His scent rose up to greet her, and she snuggled down deeper into the fleece lining. She felt like a child—free, safe, cared for. Breaking off a pointed icicle from above the doorway, she sucked on it as she admired the winter wonderland scene.

"You look like a little girl," Luke said as he stepped up behind her.

"I feel like a little girl," she answered. "I feel free."

She held out the icicle and Luke took an exaggerated lick with his tongue. "Me, too," he said.

Luke wrapped his arms around her, pulled her body to his and kissed the side of her neck. He rested his chin on top of her head. In silence they stared at the natural beauty of their surroundings. The air was crisp and clean, and the snow a blinding white. A light breeze sifted through the trees and Alex caught a chill. She noticed Luke only wore his flannel shirt.

"You must be cold," she said. "Here, take your jacket. I'll run in and get my own."

Despite his objections, she shrugged out of his jacket. As she did, a small black cylinder fell from his pocket into the snow. Both Alex and Luke bent over at the same time to retrieve it. Alex's hand reached it first.

"What's this?" she asked.

Luke stopped cold. "Film."

"Oh. You took pictures? What of?"

He reached over and plucked the cylinder out of her palm. "Scenery shots," he said, and stuffed the roll into his jeans pocket as he disappeared inside the cabin. A split second later, he returned with her fake fur. "Here," he said, thrusting her jacket at her, "I'll trade you."

They exchanged jackets and slipped into them. Luke held out his hand to Alex, and they started off in the direction of the downward slope in the road. The going was awkward, as the snow had drifted, making some spots knee-high.

They walked for about a half hour, passing two other cabins on the way. Both were snow-covered and empty. The lower the road dipped, the more snow they had to contend with. Alex kept slipping, as her boots were more for show than snow. More than once, she almost dragged Luke down with her.

"This isn't such a good idea," Luke said when they stopped to rest. "Maybe only one of us should go."

"Yes," Alex said. "Me."

"No way. I'll go on. You go back to the cabin."

"Luke, be sensible. We have no way of knowing where this road leads to, if it leads anywhere at all. You can't keep trudging through the snow with the condition your knee is in."

"I can cover more area than you," he argued.

"Maybe so. But what if you can't get back?"

She had a point. He may be able to make it down all right, but back up would be a problem. If this road led to nowhere, he'd be stuck.

Alex stepped up and put her arms around his middle. "Let's go back to the cabin. Please," she said.

Luke wrapped his arms around her. He leaned down and kissed her. She felt so good, he nuzzled her neck before reluctantly releasing her.

"The snow *is* melting," he said, more to convince himself than her.

"One more day won't matter," she added, secretly willing him to agree. She wanted to go back to the cabin. She wanted another night with him to cement the growing feelings between them.

"Okay," he said, and Alex breathed a sigh of relief. "Let's go back. If they're checking around by helicopter, they'll see the smoke from the chimney if we keep the fire going." Alex smiled, and he kissed the tip of her nose. "Does that make you happy?" She nodded. "You know something? I think you just want my body back on that mattress, that's what I think."

Alex bit his chin lightly, then brushed her mouth against his. "Hmm. That depends. What do you have to offer?" she asked.

"How easy we forget."

"I haven't forgotten. But we *are* out of condoms. We used them all up last night."

Luke grinned, a very slow, very sensual grin. "There *are* other ways to make love, Alexandra," he said.

The light in his eyes had a mischievous glow. She smiled at him coyly. "I wouldn't know about that. Being an innocent virgin and all. You'll have to explain what you mean."

"I'd much rather show you."

"Then what are we waiting for?" she asked.

Luke took hold of her hand and hauled her around. They made it back up the hill in half the time it took to get down it. Laughing and out of breath, they almost fell over the threshold of the cabin.

The fire was still blazing, and the room was warm as toast. To Alex, it was like coming home. She threw off her jacket, and quickly undressed. Naked, she put her hands together in a mock dive and jumped onto the mattress. Luke watched her, shaking his head in tolerant disbelief at her antics. Lounging on her side, one leg seductively crossed over the other, Alex opened her arms to him.

"Aren't you going to feed me first?" Luke asked.

Alex shook her head.

"I'm hungry," he said.

"So am I." She patted the space next to her. "I'm waiting for my instructions, Mr. Stratten."

"You are, are you?"

"Yes, I am. Unless you've misled me. Maybe you really don't know other ways to make love."

"Oh, I know them, all right."

"Then . . . keep your promise."

Luke dropped his jacket onto the floor. With purposeful slowness, he took off his shirt, unzipped his jeans and stepped out of them and his boots at the same time. His weight dipped into the mattress, and he lay down beside her. Without touching, Luke leaned forward and kissed her so tenderly, her insides twisted with a bittersweet pain.

"I want to make love with you. One more time, sweetheart, before we go," he whispered.

"Show me how," she said softly.

He pulled her to him, his hands roaming up, down, all over her body. "Lesson number one," he said, kissing her behind the ear, on her cheek, and down to the soft dip between her collarbone.

"Mmm," she murmured. "I see." She kissed his neck, and bit his shoulder as she ran her fingernails down his back. "Is this what you mean?"

"Very good," he said as he continued to touch every inch of her with his hands.

"Show me more," she pleaded.

"Lesson number two."

Luke's hand trailed down her belly, where he threaded his fingers through her nest of red curls. He caressed her with a gentle scratching that made her call his name out loud. Her legs parted of their own volition, and Luke wasted no time in replying to her silent invitation. He rotated his thumb over that very special spot he'd come to know as her most sensitive.

Alex moaned as his fingers dipped into her. "Oh, yes," she said, arching her back to give him access to all of her.

She turned into his touch, using her hands to explore his body, as well. When she wrapped her fingers around his hard length, Luke shuddered.

"Am I doing it correctly?" she asked with breathy innocence.

"You're definitely on the right track."

"Go on," she said. "What's lesson number three?"

"Do you think you can handle it?" he asked.

"If you can, I can," she answered.

"Okay, here goes."

Luke's mouth replaced his hands as he made his way down her body, tasting her, nipping her, licking every soft inch of her along the way. Then he kissed her intimately, his tongue slowly feasting on and around her special spot. Alex arched her body off the mattress and screamed his name in surprise at the suddenness and intensity of the sensations his mouth and tongue evoked. She grabbed handfuls of his hair and tugged in tandem to each uninhibited undulation of her body. A blinding climax caught her and took her for the roller coaster ride of her life. She fell back, limp, her heart beating triple time.

She felt as if she had died and gone to heaven.

"Oh, yes," she said once she found her voice again. "I *most definitely* like lesson number three."

Luke chuckled. Alex smiled. She felt satiated and so very good about herself. The pleased looked on his face also made her very, very confident.

"Now, it's your turn," she said, and rolled him over onto his back.

Slowly, stealthily, Alex moved over him, mimicking his actions. "Am I getting this right?" she asked as she ran her tongue across his chest, his flat male nipples, all the while zeroing in on the source of his desire.

Luke muttered his approval as he rubbed a hand across her back. But when she took him into her mouth, his entire body stiffened with delight. As she continued to show some considerable natural talent, he couldn't stop his body from reacting more swiftly than he would have liked. He entangled his fingers in her hair and tried to hold her back.

Alex tilted her head. "Something wrong?"

"I think maybe lesson number three should wait for another time," he said in a very tight voice.

"I don't think so," she said, and proceeded to pick up where she left off.

"Stop…oh, Alex…don't…Alex…don't stop."

She didn't.

* * *

Alexandra awakened to a sound. Luke slept next to her undisturbed. They had fallen into an exhausted sleep after what had to be close to a half day of non-stop lovemaking. She glanced out the window. Light still streamed in, but the directions of the rays had changed. It was late afternoon. She waited for the sound to repeat itself, but it did not.

Slowly, carefully, so as not to awaken Luke, Alex slipped off the mattress. She dressed quickly, peeking out the windows as she did. There was nothing unusual going on. She grabbed her jacket and headed out the door, shutting it gently behind her.

The cold air stimulated her as she made her way down the road. Snow crunched beneath her feet, and Alex held on to the branches of bushes and trees to keep her balance. She stopped when she heard a noise up ahead. Attempting to orient herself, she listened intently, then followed the sound.

As she passed one of the other cabins, she saw a man in a ski suit circling it.

"Who are you?" he called down to her from the cabin's front porch.

"Who are *you?*" she asked in return.

"Alexandra!"

Alex spun around at the sound of her name. She couldn't believe her eyes. Behind her, climbing the hill, were at least a half dozen men towing all sorts of rescue equipment, and one other slightly portly but very familiar man right smack-dab in the middle of them all....

"Daddy!"

Ten

Before she could assimilate what was happening, Alexandra was wrapped in a bear hug that robbed her of her breath. Her father had never been an overly demonstrative man, and the emotional embrace took her almost as much by surprise as his presence on the mountain.

Without hesitation, she reached around his ample middle and squeezed tightly in return. He felt so solid and strong, all her little girl feelings toward him quickly rose to the surface. She hadn't realized, until this moment, how truly frightening the entire experience had been.

"I thought I'd lost you," Victor Beck said, his voice muffled with uncharacteristic emotion.

"Oh, Daddy. I'm so glad to see you." As they held each other, a light went on in her head. Alex pulled back. "How did you know where I was?"

"Not now, Alexandra. Let's talk about that back at the resort. Come along. We have a couple of ATV's parked down below." With a quick hand signal to a rescue team worker, Victor took hold of her arm and started back down the hill.

"No, wait!" Alex pulled back. "There's someone else with me." She pointed up the path in the direction of the cabin. "A man," she continued. "He, uh, his knee is hurt. I don't know if he can make it all the way down the hill on his own."

"The rest of the team will go up for him," Victor said. "Come along, Alexandra."

"Daddy, no. I can't just leave him here. H-he, he's..."

"Yes?"

"He saved my life."

Victor Beck scrutinized his daughter for a long moment. "Did he *really?*" Her father's famous sarcasm was as heavy as the wet snow on the trees.

"Yes, he did. Really."

"I assume we're talking about the same man? Lucas Stratten?"

"Yes, do you know him?"

"I know of him. The question is, do you know who he is?"

"He's a reporter."

"A *tabloid* reporter. He was following you."

"I know. He told me. How did you find me, Daddy?"

"A man by the name of Joe Ryan called me. If I would agree to an exclusive interview, he would tell me where you were...and with whom. It seems the tabloid was paying Mr. Stratten's way and was notified by the resort of his disappearance. Ryan called me immediately. He wasn't about to pass up a more sensational story for a mediocre one.''

"And you agreed?" Alex asked, irritated that her father would even negotiate with this Ryan.

"Of course, I agreed! I had no idea where you were. I was worried sick about you. You go off and running, right before the wedding. What was I to think? I wanted my daughter back. When I called the resort and found out you were caught in an avalanche, I went . . . went—"

"Ballistic."

"Yes. I flew up here immediately and organized the rescue effort. Brought in my own people for the job. The damn storm kept us from setting out sooner. Now, come along." He pulled her hand. "It's cold, and I can tell you're exhausted. Have you eaten anything?"

"Yes, luckily we found shelter. The cabin was well stocked." Alex tugged at his arm again. "Daddy, I can't leave Luke up there. Let me go with the rescue team to get him."

"Why all this concern for a reporter, Alexandra? You hate reporters."

"He's not like all the rest. He told me all about himself. He free-lances, and travels all around the world doing investigative pieces."

"Bravo for him. Did he also tell you he has sold your story to the yellowest, dirtiest rag in the business?"

"He's not going to give them the story. He promised me."

Victor squinted his eyes at his daughter. "And you believe him?"

"I do."

"You've never been naive about these things before, Alex. What happened—" he motioned his head in the direction of the cabin "—up there in the last two days?"

Alex hesitated. There was only so much one should tell fathers about this sort of thing. "Nothing happened. We talked, that's all. He told me all about the story, and he said he wasn't going to use it."

"What about the photographs?" Victor asked.

"What photographs?"

"The *nude* photos of you in a hot tub that are going to grace the front page along with the story of your rescue. Did he say he wasn't going to use them, either?"

"There are no photos, Daddy. Where did you get that idea?"

"From Ryan. He told me all about his deal with Stratten. He's a *photo*journalist, Alexandra. Or did he fail to mention that part of it?"

Alex felt every hair follicle on her body rise to attention as she recalled the roll of film he had virtually snatched out of her hand only this morning. She'd asked him if he'd told her all of it...

"Yes, I guess he did forget to mention that one bit of information," she mumbled, almost to herself.

Victor took hold of her arm again. "Can we go now? My feet are freezing standing in this snow. We'll talk more back at the hotel, and you can tell me the whole story."

"The cabin," she said, almost in a daze as he pulled her along.

"What about it?"

"It needs to be cleaned...restocked. The owners—"

"For heaven's sake, Alex. We'll take care of that, of course." He urged her on, muttering as he led the way, "What a thing to worry about."

Alex followed as her father pulled her along. She glanced over her shoulder in the direction of the cabin. The rescue team was setting off with a first-aid kit and a stretcher. She thought of how Luke would feel when he was awakened by these men, how he would wonder where she was, what had happened to her.

Then a new picture formed in her mind, one of another Luke crouched down, hidden, ogling her through the eye of a camera, snapping away as she'd eased herself into the hot tub....

How could he?

Alexandra bit her lip to stop the tears from flowing. She swallowed her hurt, her anger, her fear, and obediently walked behind her father farther down the hill. The cold stung her cheeks and made her hands tingle...but as the depth of Luke's betrayal began to sink deeper into her psyche, nothing could compare with the burning, numbing ice that was forming around her heart.

If they didn't let him out of this damned straitjacket soon, he'd explode. Luke twisted and turned on the stretcher as the rescue team carried him down the hill to safety.

"I can walk," he shouted for the tenth time.

The two men ignored him and continued trudging down the hill, bumping and bouncing him every inch of the way.

"I don't need to be carried," he added. "You can let me down now."

Silence.

"Argh!"

He shut his eyes and laid his head back against the tiny pillow. Where was Alex? he wondered for the umpteenth time since the rescue workers had stormed into the cabin like commandos on a raid. All they would tell him is that she was all right and on her way back to the resort.

Why hadn't she waited for him? It didn't make any sense. One minute they were making love and the next he was being hauled down the hill like a sack of potatoes.

The ride back to the resort was no better than the trip down the hill. The only thing he had to be grateful for was the fact that he had been able to talk them into taking him back to the resort and not to a hospital as they'd originally planned. Other than that, no one seemed to know anything. The only information he could gather was that the rescue team worked for Victor Beck.

Luke gritted his teeth. He should have guessed. Who else but the almighty Victor Beck would be able to orchestrate a drama such as this? The man was probably holding a press conference right now at the bottom of the mountain outlining his single-handed rescue of his poor, frightened daughter and her companion. That is, if he even bothered to mention Luke at all. Probably would just as soon forget the obscure reporter who had saved Alex's life.

Not that he wanted any credit for it. He'd do it all again a hundred times over if only to spend those hours and days with her. Her face, bathed in firelight and ecstasy, came into view in his mind's eye. No, not a hundred times. A thousand. More.

His stomach dropped when they hit a dip in the road, and it brought him back to reality. As the resort came into view, the ATV slowed down as it wound its way around the drive to the front entrance. People swarmed the vehicle to stare inside, some with cameras snapping pictures of him trussed up like Tom Turkey just before Thanksgiving dinner.

"Get them out of here!" he shouted to the team workers. Again, they ignored him. What were these guys? Robots?

The ATV finally came to a stop, and the back doors swung open to allow the rescuers to pull Luke off his stretcher and onto a waiting gurney.

"This is getting a bit ridiculous, guys," he said as they worked on him. "I can walk. Believe me when I tell you."

The ride through the lobby was almost as humiliating as the trip in the ATV. Strangers hovered over him asking questions that he had no intention of answering. All he wanted to do was get off this thing and find Alex. Luke told himself they'd leave him alone once they got him in his room and on his bed. He tried to hold on to his temper for a few moments more, and almost succeeded until he saw Victor Beck standing in the center of the common room in the midst of a gaggle of reporters.

That did it.

With strength he didn't know he had, Luke freed his arms from the restraints and shimmied his legs out of the confines. With the gurney still heading for the elevator, he hopped off, much to the surprise of the worker who had been pulling him along.

"Thanks for the ride," he said with a quick salute.

His leg was stiff, but he was able to walk over to the group assembled in the center of the room.

"Mr. Beck," he called.

The crowd turned to look at him. Slowly, a path was cleared to allow his stilted but purposeful gait right up to the man who was obviously in charge of this charade.

"Where is she?" Luke asked.

Victor Beck eyed Luke warily. His eyes squinted as he slowly, almost insultingly, examined Luke from head to toe. "You're Luke Stratten, aren't you?"

"You know damn well who I am, Beck. Now where is she?"

"Now you don't think I'm really going to let you see her, do you?" Beck said, to the glory of the reporters who were taking in every word on paper, video and film.

"You have no control over her. She's an adult, and I guarantee you she does want to see me."

"Dream on, Stratten. My daughter is on her way back to New York on my personal jet. She has much to do to prepare for her forthcoming wedding."

"Wedding? What are you talking about?" Luke asked, cold dread fingering its way through his system. "She's not marrying Farrell. She swore it."

"I'm sure she would have said anything in that threatening situation. Whatever the case, the truth is that Alexandra has agreed to reschedule her marriage to Justin Farrell for as soon as the arrangements can be made."

"I don't believe you."

"I really don't care what you believe." Victor Beck turned from Luke, dismissing him with his body language.

"I'll find her myself," Luke said, and stormed past the hovering reporters as he pushed his way through the lobby and up to the front desk.

"Is Ms. Beck still here?" he asked the clerk.

"No, sir. I was told she left for the airport in Mr. Beck's helicopter soon after she was rescued. We're forwarding her things."

Luke muttered an expletive. "Are there any messages for me?" he asked.

"Oh, yes. A Mr. Joe Ryan has been quite frantic about you. He said you were to call him the moment you returned."

Luke grabbed the pink slip from the man. "Yeah, I know to call Joe. Any other messages? Like from Ms. Beck?"

The clerk shook his head. "No, I'm sorry, sir. No other messages."

Luke exhaled a deep breath, then nodded at the clerk. Ignoring the stares of the people milling around the lobby, he pocketed his room key and made his way to the elevators and his room. Once inside, he dropped down on the bed and ran a hand through his hair.

What had happened? What could possibly have changed Alexandra's mind from one moment to the next? Beck was lying, that was the only possible explanation for all of this. He'd spirited Alex away on some false pretense, and stopped her from leaving a message for him. That had to be it.

She had feelings for him. She'd given herself to him. It had been her first time, her gift, and she had given it to *him*. He didn't care how jaded she was or how socially inept he was, he'd learned enough about her in two days to know that they'd shared something very, very special, something she wouldn't walk away from so easily, especially into the arms of another man.

The thought of someone else touching her made his stomach churn and his blood boil.

She wouldn't do it.

She couldn't.

The Alex he knew was *his*.

The Alex he knew. That was the problem. What if her father was right? What if she'd promised the moon while they were locked away in that cabin only to think differently in the light of day? He had been the reluctant one, after all. She had professed her love, or at least said she had been *thinking* about it. He had been the one to put her off with his tale of confusion and undependable life-style. What if she took all he'd said to heart? What if she thought it would be better to just disappear out of his life without so much as a by-your-leave?

He would deserve it, if she did just that, he told himself. All she'd wanted this morning was some reassurance, some small crumb of hope that they could make a life together. Instead, all she'd gotten for her effort was that old reliable facade he'd always fallen back on when someone got too close, when he began to care too much.

Like now.

He squeezed his eyes shut. God, he cared, so deeply it was imbedded in his soul. He couldn't imagine not seeing her again. Couldn't even dream of not touching her, kissing her, burying himself in her ever again.

Ever again was a long, long time—

The knock startled him. He rose and leaned toward the door. "Who is it?"

"Victor Beck."

Luke opened the door and Alex's father stepped inside.

"What do you want?" he asked the older man.

"How much?" Beck asked in return.

"How much for what?"

"The photos. The naked pictures of my daughter. How much do you want for them?"

"How did you know—?"

Victor waved him off with his hand. "I'm not here to quibble with you, Stratten. I don't want to see my daughter plastered on the front page of every sleazy tabloid in the world. Just name your price. I'll match whatever Ryan offered you. I'll double it."

"Joe called you?"

"Of course, he called me. How do you think I found Alexandra?"

"I don't know. Private detectives?"

"They don't work as well as people think. Especially when someone doesn't want to be found. Alexandra didn't." He took a step forward. "Again, I ask. How much?"

Luke stared at the ceiling and spun around. "They're not for sale. Not at any price."

"Don't be ridiculous, Stratten. I know you need money. Ryan told me the whole story. I'm offering you double what he would pay you. Don't be stubborn."

"I'm not being stubborn. I meant what I said. The photographs are not for sale. Not to you. Not to Joe. Not to anybody."

"You're not going to sell them at all?"

"No."

"Why not?"

"My business."

"I beg to differ. The pictures are of my daughter. They are very much my business."

"Where is Alex? I need to speak to her."

"She doesn't want to see you. She was very explicit about that," Victor said.

"She knows about the photographs?"

"Yes. I told her. Didn't you think she'd find out?"

Luke hesitated, then shook his head. "No, I didn't." He laughed, a mirthless, derisive sound. "*That* was pretty stupid, wasn't it?"

The question was rhetorical, and Victor chose to ignore it. "If you aren't going to sell the pictures, then give them to me."

"No. They're mine. I'm keeping them."

"What could you possibly want them for?" Victor asked.

Luke smiled, a slow, sad smile. "Souvenirs."

His bags were packed, and he stashed them near the doorway as he waited for the van. He'd showered and changed, called Joe, and even tried to take a quick nap, but that hadn't worked out. He was wound tight, and his mind was racing in a thousand different directions.

His main objective right now was to get back to New York as fast as he could. Once there, he had no idea what would happen next. There was still Africa. Though it seemed like a lifetime, in reality only two days had passed. He could reschedule his flight and worry about paying for it later.

But then, there was Alexandra. Could he really leave the country with all this unresolved between them? Could he go away and let her marry Farrell? Could he walk away from all this without a glance back? No, if nothing else, he had to see her before he left. He had to give her the opportunity to tell him to his face that she was marrying someone else. She owed him that much.

The temperature had dropped, and his breath smoked up the air around him. He hunched farther into the fleece collar of his jacket and wondered what the hell he was going to do.

"Psst."

Luke turned. There was no one there.

"Over here."

He followed the direction of the sound and saw a hand dart out from behind a column on the other side of the doorway. Luke glanced left and right, then walked over to the column.

"Who is it?" Luke asked.

"It's me. Tony. You know, the snowmobile guy."

"Oh, yeah. Tony. How are you?" Luke asked, glancing toward the driveway in search of the van.

"Didn't believe me, did you?" Tony asked.

"About what?"

"The snowstorm. I told you."

"Yeah," Luke said. "You sure did."

"I have something else to tell you, too," he said.

"What is it?"

"It'll cost you."

"Sorry, man. I'm broke."

"Ah, what the hell," Tony said. "I'll tell you, anyway." He leaned forward. "You know that lady you were stuck with?"

"Alexandra?"

"Yeah. Her. Well, she's still here."

"Here? At the resort? No way. She took off this afternoon in her daddy's helicopter. Probably in New York by now."

"Don't bet on it," Tony said. "They just said that to throw off the press. She'd still here. In the same villa."

Luke gave him a wary look. "No joke?"

"No joke. I saw her. She's here."

Luke looked around. The place was deserted. Once the press left, the rest of the people just drifted away. He checked his watch. It was the dinner hour, and most of the guests would be heading for the dining room.

"Keep an eye on that stuff for me?" Luke asked Tony, pointing to his luggage.

"No problem," Tony said as Luke headed in the direction of the villas. "Go get her."

Alexandra was moping. She had never been this physically tired in her life, yet she couldn't shut her eyes for more than ten seconds at a time. The satin sheets on the bed felt cool and silky against her skin, but the mattress seemed too soft after sleeping on the floor for two days.

Restless, she rose and padded to the vanity table where she sat and brushed her hair. It had felt gloriously decadent to take a long, hot bath and wash her hair, and the dinner that Daddy had ordered had been fit for a queen. Yet she had hardly touched the artfully arranged cuisine. Daddy had asked if she was feeling all right. She'd reassured him that she was just tired, but that was not the entire truth. She was sick—heartsick.

How could he do it? She asked herself that question over and over again ad nauseam. He'd been so gentle, tender, loving with her, she'd been so sure that he was feeling something deep down. Even though the words were missing, he'd spoken volumes with his hands, his lips, the strength and passion of his body.

It couldn't have been a lie. She had made poor decisions where men were concerned in the past, but she wasn't that bad a judge of character, was she? All of this recrimination was driving her crazy. Yet no matter how many excuses she made for his behavior, the facts remained. Daddy had even gone to see him to get the film back, but he had refused to turn it over.

What did he plan to do with the photos? She put her head in her hands. This would be much worse than the nursing school fiasco. These wouldn't be doctored. These would be real, in-the-flesh, naked pictures of her. She had no doubt that they were clear, professional and close-up. In the short time she'd spent with Luke, she'd come to realize that he was damn good at anything he tried to do. If it had been anyone else who'd taken those pictures, she'd be humiliated, but she'd survive it. But Luke...

God, how it hurt. She'd given him every opportunity to tell her everything. Why hadn't he mentioned the pictures if he wasn't planning to use them? She knew how much he needed the money for his African trip. But Daddy had offered him money, more than the tabloid, and he still wouldn't turn the film over. There had to be another reason.

She looked up and caught her reflection in the mirror. Blackmail? Could that be it? Of course! Why sell the pictures once when he could dangle them in front of her over and over again, financing any and all future expeditions for as long as he needed?

The pain in her middle was becoming so unbearable, she had to double over in the seat. She fought back the tears that threatened once again, but couldn't stifle the moan that forced its way out of her throat.

A tapping sound broke her reverie. Alexandra rose and walked toward the patio doors. The heavy draperies were shut tightly for the night. She insinuated her hand into the opening and peered outside into the darkness.

She jumped back at the sight of Luke's face on the other side of the pane.

"Let me in," he said, his voice muted from the separation of glass.

"Go away."

"Alexandra, open the door."

"No."

"I'm standing on a ledge here. If you don't open the door, I'll fall off."

"You can fall off the edge of the earth for all I care."

"Alex—"

She shut the draperies and walked away. How dare he come here looking for her! How dare he even show his face to her after all the lying—

She heard a rustling sound, then a thump. Alexandra moved closer to the draperies. She shut one eye to peek through the slit. He was gone. Or so it seemed. She opened the draperies a bit more, and sure enough, he was nowhere to be seen. She looked to the right and left, and was just about to shut the draperies altogether when a crash on the other side of the room spun her around.

Alex put her hand to her mouth. "Oh!"

Luke had knocked over a small table as he dangled half in, half out the window on the opposite wall.

"Ouch!" He'd hit his knee on the sill. "I could use a hand here," he said as he tried to get his other too long leg through the small opening.

"Why should I help you? You're a liar and a cheat," she said, hand on hip.

"You don't believe that," he said as he finally completed his mission.

As he advanced on her, she retreated. "Don't come any closer. I'll scream."

Luke reached out and grabbed hold of her upper arms. "Go ahead," he said as his head descended, "scream."

When his lips met hers, Alex melted inside and out. She swayed into him as if on command. He parted her lips with his tongue, searing her with his heat and longing with every touch.

Helplessly, she groaned and wrapped her arms around his neck, clinging to his hair, breathing in the fresh, clean, familiar scent of him. His hands reached down to cup her buttocks, and he pressed her up into his aroused body, nestling her in just the right spot to drive them both crazy for more.

"I had to know," he said into her mouth, "if it was real, or if I dreamed it."

"Oh, Luke," she said, asking the one question that plagued her, "how could you?"

"I didn't think you'd find out about the pictures."

"How could I not find out? Once they were published—"

"I had no intention of selling them. I told your father that. Didn't he tell you?"

"Yes, but then, why won't you give them to us?"

Luke broke away from her. He wondered that himself. But for some stubborn reason, he felt the pictures were his. He'd changed his plans for them. He'd lost his camera equipment for them. Hell, he'd risked his life for them. He wouldn't sell them, but he wanted to keep them. They were too special to part with. Only he knew what they represented to him. Only he knew how she'd looked when he'd first seen her through the eye of his camera, and as far as he was concerned, only *he* would ever know.

"I won't sell them, Alexandra. I promise."

Alex shook her head. "Not good enough," she said. "I need to know what you're going to do with them."

"Keep them."

"For what purpose?" she asked.

Luke took a step back. "What do you mean?"

"I want to know your intentions."

"I have no intentions," he said.

"None?"

"Spit it out, Alex," he said, anger apparent in his voice. "What intentions could I have?"

Alex felt the power of his pent-up fury, but pushed on. She needed to know. "Blackmail."

Luke felt a surge of blood rush to his head with the force of a tidal wave. If she were a man, he would have punched her out for even thinking it let alone accusing him of something so vile. Instead he stepped back toward the open window and clenched his fists to avoid reaching out to her.

"Is that what you think?" he asked, his voice deep and dark with untold emotions.

Alex swallowed. "It's a possibility that's crossed my mind."

He shook his head. "You don't know me at all, do you?" *And I don't know you.*

"Luke—"

"No," he said emphatically. "Maybe I ought to think about it. Blackmail. It never crossed *my* mind, but maybe it should have. I *do* need the money, as you and your father keep reminding me. It's something to think about. Maybe I'll wait until after your wedding, then I can hit up your old man *and* your new husband at the same time. Double the money, double the fun."

He turned and began to climb back out the window.

"Luke, don't leave like this. Let's talk—"

"There's nothing left to talk about, is there?" He gave her a quick salute. "Thanks for the memories, as they say." He made it out onto the ledge, then turned and poked his head inside for one last look. The pain in his chest was intense, so he lashed out in the only way he knew how. "And, oh, congratulations. Remember me to your husband on your wedding night."

Alex ran to the window. Panicked, she called out his name several times, but there was no answer.

Just as quickly as Luke Stratten had entered her life, he'd disappeared.

Eleven

——

Alexandra stared out the window of her Fifth Avenue apartment. The view was magnificent, the best the city had to offer. Central Park was in bloom with the celery green promise of spring and budding May flowers. The street vendors were busy hawking their wares to the continuous stream of people who hustled to and fro on their way to do their daily business.

She lifted her face into a ray of sunlight and shut her eyes as she absorbed the welcome warmth.

"Do you want to take this robe along with you?"

Alex turned to see her maid, Calinda, holding up a royal blue Oriental silk robe her father had brought her back from China.

"Yes, please pack it," she said. "I can use it by the pool."

Alex checked her dresser for the umpteenth time to be sure she'd packed all her makeup essentials. Not that she'd need them. She planned to stay put and out of sight most of the time. She was off to Daddy's house in the Hamptons to rest, relax . . . and forget.

The two months since her "mountain escapade," as the media continued to refer to her time with Luke, had been spent trying to elude the press. For the first few weeks, she'd held her breath in anticipation of the nude photographs showing up somewhere or other. When they didn't, she'd fallen back into the uncomfortable state of waiting for the next shoe to drop. But then, maybe Luke had meant what he'd said . . . at least about the photographs.

That didn't mean the New York reporters were giving her a free ride. Victor's announcement that she had reconsidered her plans to marry Justin Farrell had only fueled the press's already maniacal pursuit of anything and everything to do with Alexandra Beck.

Luke had gotten off lucky. She hadn't heard from him since he'd disappeared from the room of her villa the night they'd been rescued. She told herself she didn't care. He was a liar, and who knew what else.

But her heart told another story.

Unable to stop herself, she'd swallowed her pride and called Joe Ryan to find out where he was. It seemed he'd wasted no time borrowing money from Joe and catching that plane to Africa the day after their rescue. As far as she knew, he hadn't returned.

Alexandra was determined to stop this pining. The situation was impossible, had been from the very beginning. After all, in reality she'd only known the man two days out of her life. He shouldn't be consuming her thoughts this way. It was time to take some action, to tie up loose ends and put this all behind her.

The past two months she had been busy interviewing managers for her foundation. It was amazing how much work was involved in giving money away. She'd had to find office space, hire staff, and study endless grant requests from charity organizations. As time-consuming as this business was, she was grateful for the work. It had forced her to think about something other than herself . . . other than Luke.

But now she needed to get away. She had been neglecting herself. She'd lost weight, and her friends were pushing her to go to the Caribbean for a rest. Alex didn't want to be that far away from her fledgling organization, so she'd compromised and chosen the famous little strip of paradise along the southern coast of Long Island instead.

There had been only one last loose end to tie up and that had been Justin Farrell. The poor man had been bounced around more times than a tennis ball at the U.S. Open. Last night she had remedied that situation by having dinner with him and explaining that she could never marry him. He was understanding and very gracious, and if she didn't know better, she might even say relieved.

This morning's papers, however, had told another tale. A photo of she and Justin looking very cozy at the restaurant last night graced the gossip columns of the major New York papers, fueling speculation that the wedding was "on" again.

"All done," Calinda said. "Do you want me to have the bags put in the car?"

"Yes, please," Alex said. "I'm leaving in a few minutes."

Calinda walked toward the door with a suitcase in her hand. "Oh, I meant to tell you. Your father called early this morning. He wants you to come to his office.''

''Did he say what about?''

''No, miss. He just said for you to stop by on your way to the Island.''

''Thank you, Calinda.''

The maid nodded and exited the room. Now, what could that be all about? She'd spoken to Daddy last night. He'd tried to talk her out of going. He'd said she was hiding away and that it was unhealthy. Maybe so, she'd said, but she needed time alone. She wondered what he wanted to see her about that couldn't wait.

In a strange way, the experience in the mountains had done more than ''make her a woman.'' It had matured her, forced her to focus on what was truly important to her. She didn't know where to go from here. The work on the Alexandra Beck Foundation had begun, but the work on Alexandra Beck, the person, still had a long way to go.

Like it or not, she had fallen in love with a stubborn, independent, unreliable, commitment-fearing *reporter.* Out of all the men in the world—and in many ways, she'd had all of them to choose from—she had picked this totally unsuitable one.

Memories of him swirled around her day and night. The touch of his hand, the taste of his kisses, the power of his body on and in hers, kept her sleepless and helpless to go forward. Her life seemed to be divided into two parts—B.L., Before Luke, and A.L., After Luke. She had cried over him so much she was surprised there was still any discernible amount of water left in her body.

Love hurts, she told herself over and over again, particularly one-sided love with the wrong man. But all the recriminations in the world didn't change the fact that she longed for him every minute of every day in the most elemental way possible.

Her father couldn't understand it, and she couldn't explain. She just knew it was so. She also knew only *she* could end it. The best way to get over him was to go somewhere that would totally disassociate her from anything that reminded her of Lucas Stratten.

Like the beach. A wide-open, high-ceilinged, beach house in May would be the perfect antidote to a tiny, one-room, rustic cabin in the snowy Vermont mountains.

Alexandra picked up her purse and headed toward the door. Anxious to be on her way, she thought about Daddy's unplanned request, then mentally shrugged. One more stop to make, she told herself.

Traffic was the typical midday New York nightmare as Alex squeezed her red Corvette into the line of vehicles. She glanced into each of the fashionable department store windows as she inched south on Fifth Avenue toward her father's office. The artistically arranged summer apparel displays put her in the mood for her trip.

Once there, the doorman took her car, a luxury she never failed to appreciate in a city where parking spaces were more precious than gold. She rode the elevator to the top floor and exited into the private office wing that housed Victor Beck's billion-dollar empire.

Alexandra waved to the receptionist as she took her time walking through the familiar mahogany maze to her father's spacious office. The room never ceased to astonish her. Situated in the corner of the building, it had ceiling-to-floor glass walls on two sides, which created the breathtaking illusion of walking on air.

Her father was on the phone and indicated she should sit. She chose an oversize leather swivel chair to the right of his desk and spun herself in the direction of the glass wall. The city enveloped her. From up here everything looked miniature perfect, calm, even safe.

Appearances, she knew, were deceiving.

"All set to leave?" Victor asked as he hung up the phone.

"Yes. I was on my way when Calinda gave me your message. What's this all about, Daddy?"

"This," he said, and handed her a short, handwritten note on wrinkled, recycled paper.

Alex quickly read the note. It was a request for a "business" meeting. Her heart flip-flopped in her chest at the sight of Luke's signature. "I don't believe it."

"He's due here momentarily. I thought you'd want to be present."

"Why now?"

"I assume he needs the money."

"He needed the money before. There must be something else."

"Alexandra, don't read anything more into this than what there is. I told him I'd double any offer he'd received on the photographs. He probably has decided he's ready to deal. Probably will up the ante, as well."

"He had his chance to—"

Victor cut her off with the wave of his hand. "Why else would he contact me? I don't mean to be cruel, my dear, but if he'd wanted to see you, he would have called you directly."

Before Alex could think of a suitable rebuttal, the sound of the intercom intruded. "Mr. Beck? A Mr. Stratten to see you," the receptionist announced.

"Send him in." Victor snapped the button off. "Let me do the talking," he said to Alexandra.

Luke stopped outside the office door. He was forcing himself to do this. The photographs were like a burr in his boot, a constant, irritating reminder of what had become, in his mind, an impossible dream. Better to get rid of them, he'd told himself a hundred times. Yet he couldn't bring himself to destroy them. It almost seemed as if he'd be hurting Alexandra herself.

Since he couldn't do it himself, there was only one other person he could trust them with: Victor Beck. As unappealing as it was to deal with the man, Luke felt it was the best, safest, course of action to rid himself of what was fast becoming an addiction.

He'd stupidly taken the photographs to Africa with him. At odd times of the day or night, they seemed to call out to him, haunt him, beckon him...and he would always give in. He'd slip one or more of the photos out of his hiding place in his knapsack and stare at them, remembering the way her skin felt against his, the taste of every delicious morsel of her. The trip had been hard, the story cruel, but the torment he carried around inside him surpassed any and all passion he could have put into his work.

It had to end. Luke shook his head as if to clear it, and reached for the knob.

The door opened, and he walked in. Alexandra had forgotten how tall he was, how handsome, and how his presence completely filled a room. He was thinner, very tanned, and looked as if he'd just stepped out of a Banana Republic catalogue. Her heart was in her throat, but she managed to keep her face neutral. She swiveled the chair in his direction.

Luke took a second step into the room and stopped dead. His gut twisted. He hadn't expected to see her. He had purposely written to Victor in hopes that he could avoid any contact with Alexandra at all.

But apparently that was not to be.

For the longest moment, he just stared at her. She was as beautiful as his flawed memory recalled; perhaps even more so if you factored in the sunlight streaming through the glass wall, which cast an ethereal golden glow around her. She appeared composed, unbothered, and almost serene.

He, on the other hand, was grouchy, tired, and couldn't walk very well. Africa had been . . . well, Africa—hot, dusty, and more primitive than he'd remembered. His knee had taken a beating, what with the difficult traveling conditions, squatting by open fires, and just plain endless walking he had endured in the two months he had been on assignment. He was, most definitely, getting too old for this.

"Mr. Stratten," Victor said, coming out from behind his desk with his hand extended.

Luke shook it reluctantly. This was not a pleasure call. This, as his note had said, was business.

His business.

"Don't I get a hello?" Alex asked, amazed at how calm her voice sounded. She rose and stood next to her father to face Luke. He looked tired, but wonderful to her starved eyes. Too wonderful.

Luke shifted his weight onto his good leg. "Ms. Beck."

"Oh, I think we're beyond Ms. and Mr., don't you, Luke?" she asked. "I think we're certainly on a first-name basis by now."

"Alexandra," he said, and extended his hand. The word rolled off his tongue easily. Why shouldn't it? He'd been muttering it every waking hour of the day—and probably night—for the past two months. "How are you?"

Their hands touched, and Luke felt the shock dart up his arm and through his system like an electric current. He quickly let go. Alex's chin went up slightly. He recognized the defensive action.

"Fine."

"I'm surprised you're here. I thought those wedding plans of yours would be keeping you very busy about now."

"There are no wedding plans, Luke. I thought I made that perfectly clear... when was it? Two, three months ago?"

"Two," he said quietly.

"Oh, yes, two. Time flies so when one is busy," she said, and turned from him, walking to the window/wall. Her stomach was churning, and she felt the blood rise to her face. She didn't want him looking at her like that, staring at her, almost feeding on her.

"Today's papers say the wedding's back on," he said. His gut twisted again, the same way it had at the airport when he'd first seen the picture of her and Farrell in the "People" page.

She graced him with a cool glance over her shoulder. "You, of all people, should know not to believe all you read in the papers."

Their eyes met and held. Hundreds, thousands of thoughts, unresolved feelings, and might-have-beens passed between them.

Victor coughed. Luke broke eye contact with her and turned his attention to her father.

"You said you had some business to discuss," Victor said.

"Yes."

"I assume it's about the photographs."

Luke held up a large envelope. "It is."

"You have them with you?"

Alexandra's head snapped around. Luke looked at her as he answered. "Yes."

"Times must be very hard, Luke, if you're finally prepared to sell them," she said. "I remember a similar conversation when you adamantly refused."

"That was then."

"Yes. That was then," she repeated.

Tears were threatening. She swallowed a lump the size of a huge rock, and walked forward. She had to get out of here, away from him. This was a torture she wasn't prepared to bear. God help her, but the sight of him only fueled her love for him. Why? she asked. Why did he have to come back?

Alexandra picked up her purse and brushed past her father and Luke. She grabbed hold of the doorknob and swung the door open. Turning, with tears visibly pooled in her eyes, she faced both men. "Give him whatever he wants, Daddy. He was worth it."

The door slammed behind her, leaving Victor and Luke staring at its blankness. Victor moved forward to call her back, but Luke stopped him.

"Let her go," he said in a voice so resigned it caused Victor to do a double take.

"Humph. Well," Victor said, "I suppose we should get down to business."

Luke thrust the envelope out toward Victor. "The negatives are in there, as well. I developed them myself so you don't have to worry about anyone else having copies."

Victor didn't take the envelope. Instead he walked behind his desk and took out a large, ledger-size checkbook. He sat and perched his reading glasses on the tip of his nose.

"How much, Stratten?" he asked as he scratched Luke's name onto the front of a check.

"Nothing."

Victor's eyes flew up. "No money?"

"None."

"What's the meaning of this? If you don't want payment for the photographs, what do you want?"

"Peace of mind."

Victor slid the glasses away from his face and sat back. He scrutinized Luke for a very long time. Luke stood still as he did. It didn't matter whether he liked Victor Beck or not. Under the circumstances, as Alex's father, the man had a right to take his measure.

"Money can't buy you that," Victor said.

"Tell me about it."

Despite his cynicism, the thing Luke wanted most of all was the peace of mind he'd had before he'd ever set eyes on Alexandra Beck. He'd reckoned the only way to achieve that was to get Alex out of his head. Having the pictures available impeded his ability to get on with his life. So, big deal, he loved her. That was a problem he'd have to learn to live with. She could never feel the same way about him. She'd proven that with her low opinion of him. She couldn't trust him, didn't know how. He would always be just a dirty word to her—reporter.

Victor waved him forward and indicated he sit. Luke acquiesced and sat in the same chair Alex had occupied. Exhausted from his trip, he straightened out his right leg and massaged the knee.

Victor squinted his eyes. "Do you love my daughter?"

Luke stopped rubbing his knee. He looked up and held Victor's steadfast gaze. "What difference does it make?"

"Don't answer my question with a question, young man. Do you love her?"

"Yes."

A slow smile graced the older man's face. "I thought so. She loves you, too."

Luke shook his head. "No, she doesn't. She called me a liar and a cheat."

Victor laughed out loud. "That's Alex, all right. Very dramatic. Much like her mother. When I was courting Felicia, she called me a robber baron."

"She was right."

Victor laughed again. "So she was!" He stood and walked around the desk to stand over Luke. He picked up the envelope with the photographs in it and held it out to Luke. "Give these to Alex, not me. Tell her how you feel about her. I think you'll be pleasantly surprised."

Luke shook his head. "It won't work," he said. "We come from two different worlds."

Victor put his hand on Luke's shoulder. "If you really want to, you can make it one."

Luke stared at Victor Beck. "I would think you'd be the last person who would want to see us together."

"I care about my daughter. And I want her to be happy. I think you can make her that."

Luke stood, then paced in front of the desk. "Even if it were possible, I wouldn't know where to begin with her."

"Begin by telling her how you feel. She's on her way to my house in the Hamptons. She's driving. I'll arrange for my helicopter to take you. You'll get there before she does."

"Why are you doing this?" Luke asked.

"Because, contrary to what everyone says about me, Mr. Stratten—" Victor smiled his close-the-deal smile "—I really do have a heart."

It was dangerous to drive the car while crying. Alexandra found that out as soon as she'd hit the Long Island Expressway and had to pull off to the side of the road to avoid a tractor-trailer driver who didn't give a hoot that she was swerving because she had to daub her eyes with a tissue.

She'd resumed the trip only after she'd composed herself, but now her makeup was all washed off and her eyes were puffy. What did she care? There was no one to see her. She pressed her foot down harder onto the accelerator. The faster she arrived at the house, the faster she could curl up into a fetal position and cry herself to sleep.

The house was set back with a mile-long, tree-lined drive that opened into a huge, flat plateau overlooking the dunes. Contemporary in style, it was all multi-leveled wood and glass. She loved this place, and it always soothed her whenever her life wasn't going exactly as planned.

She hoped the house was up to this new challenge.

Alex left the keys and her bags in the car. Suddenly she was very tired. The strain of seeing Luke again was almost more than she could bear. All she wanted to do was undress and hide in her bed.

The front door was open, and she stepped into the airy entranceway. She wondered where George, the caretaker, was. She'd phoned him to tell him she was coming today. The house looked fresh and clean, and the windows were open to the ocean breeze.

Alex shrugged. He was probably busy doing something somewhere else on the grounds. He'd see her car soon enough and know she was here. Slowly, steadily, she climbed the curved stairway to the third level where her bedroom was located. As she approached the entrance to her suite of rooms, she heard water running. The thought that George would be considerate enough to run her a bath warmed her, and she smiled as she entered the room.

"George?" she called.

No answer.

She dropped her purse on a table and moved cautiously toward the bed. The sound of rushing water became louder.

"George? Is that you?"

The silence that greeted her prickled her skin. With trepidation, she moved closer to the adjoining bath, but turned when she noticed something on her bed. She moved closer.

Photographs.

She lifted one eight-by-ten in her hand. It was she. In the hot tub in Vermont. Her eyes were closed, her breasts peeked out above the water.

Luke's photos.

How did they get here? A chill ran down her back. Alex dropped the photo and chose another, then another still. All were different shots of the same scene, in time sequence.

For the first time she noticed the trail of clothing strewn on the floor. She walked over and picked up one item. A safari shirt. Her heart began to beat faster. She picked up the next item. Khaki pants.

That did it. She didn't need Sherlock Holmes to figure this one out. Alex stormed into the bathroom, stopping dead at the sight of Luke, eyes closed, lounging full-length in her whirlpool bath.

For the longest moment Alexandra's eyes drank in the sight. He filled the tub the way he filled a room, and her heart swelled in her chest with undeniable love. As the bubbling water caressed his broad, tanned shoulders, he opened his eyes.

"How did you get here?" she demanded.

"Alexandra. How was your drive?"

"You didn't answer my question." She knew she had to maintain control. But it wasn't easy with him large and gloriously naked just steps away from her.

"Helicopter."

"Daddy's?"

Luke nodded. "He thought I should give the pictures to you personally."

"How much did it cost him?"

"Nothing. They're yours."

"What are you saying, Luke?" she asked, her heart beating triple time in her chest.

"Get undressed and join me, and I'll tell you all about it," he said.

"Uh-uh," she said as she shook her head. "Not until you tell me what you're doing here."

"Fulfilling a fantasy."

"Luke—"

"Come on in, sweetheart, the water's warm—"

"Where's George?" she asked.

"I sent him to the store. Thought we'd eat in tonight. That all right with you?"

"Luke—"

"Alex, I'm turning into a prune."

"You can't seriously think I'm going to get in that tub with you."

"Why shouldn't you?"

"Why should I?"

Luke pushed up to a full sitting position. Droplets of water glistened in his chest hair, and Alex had to do all she could to not reach out and run her fingers through it.

"Because I want you?"

"Not good enough," she said, but her knees went weak with his words.

"Because I need you?"

Alex began to unbutton her blouse. "You're getting warmer."

"Because, sweetheart, I'm head over heels in love with you?"

That did it. Alexandra smiled from ear to ear. "Do you really mean that?"

"Get in here and I'll show you how much."

"Lesson one, two, or three?" she asked.

"Four."

Within seconds, her clothes were on the floor and Alex was up to her neck in water and cradled in his arms. She sat astride him, and found him already thoroughly aroused.

For the longest time, Luke stared into her eyes. Like a blind man, he traced each feature on her face with the tips of his fingers as he reacquainted himself with his love.

"I love you," she whispered.

And then Luke kissed her. Alex parted her lips for him, and he lost no time in exploring her mouth thoroughly with his tongue. Her stomach dropped as the center of her desire swelled and blossomed in response to his scent, his taste, the feel of his hands on her skin. The heat of the water was nothing compared to the scorching need inside her.

Luke angled his head, grabbing handfuls of her hair as he held her still while he feasted on her mouth.

"Oh, God, I missed you," Luke said as he pressed her soft body into his. "Every day, every night in Africa was hell without you."

"I'm sorry I called you a liar and a cheat."

"I'm sorry I ran out on you. I've never been one to stop and work things out. I've always dealt with my problems by running away from them." He leaned over and brushed his lips across her hairline. "No more, sweetheart. I'm here to stay, if you'll have me."

"What about your job? Your traveling?"

Luke shook his head. "It's over. The Africa story was well received. My reputation is solid. A national newsmagazine offered me a job stateside a while back. I've decided to take it."

"No more tabloid work for Ryan?" she asked.

"What do you think?" he said.

"Mmm, I don't know," Alex said as she rubbed herself against him. "I think I owe him a debt of gratitude. He is the one who brought us together."

Luke pushed a tendril of honey red hair behind her ear. "We'll ask him to be best man," he said. Alex beamed. "You like that idea?"

When she nodded, Luke lifted her above him just enough to join them together with one smooth thrust. He shut his eyes and savored the moment. It was like coming home.

Luke angled his head and nibbled at her ear. "He really had nothing to do with it, you know," he whispered, his voice hoarse with passion.

"He didn't?" Alex sighed and arched her back, moving her hips slowly to take all of him inside her.

"No," Luke said before losing himself to sensation. "All it took, sweetheart, was just one look."

*   *   *   *   *

SILHOUETTE®

Desire®

JOAN JOHNSTON'S

SERIES CONTINUES!

Available in March, *The Cowboy Takes a Wife* (D #842) is the latest addition to Joan Johnston's sexy series about the lives and loves of the irresistible Whitelaw family. Set on a Wyoming ranch, this heart-wrenching story tells the tale of a single mother who desperately needs a husband—a very *big* husband—fast!

Don't miss *The Cowboy Takes a Wife* by Joan Johnston, only from Silhouette Desire.

Relive the romance...
Harlequin and Silhouette
are proud to present

by *Request* ™

A program of collections of three complete novels by the most requested authors with the most requested themes. Be sure to look for one volume each month with three complete novels by top name authors.

In January: **WESTERN LOVING**   Susan Fox
JoAnn Ross
Barbara Kaye

Loving a cowboy is easy—taming him isn't!

In February: **LOVER, COME BACK!**   Diana Palmer
Lisa Jackson
Patricia Gardner Evans

It was over so long ago—yet now they're calling, "Lover, Come Back!"

In March: **TEMPERATURE RISING**   JoAnn Ross
Tess Gerritsen
Jacqueline Diamond

Falling in love—just what the doctor ordered!

Available at your favorite retail outlet.

REQ-G3

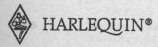
HARLEQUIN®   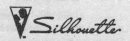Silhouette

by Ann Major

Take a walk on the wild side with Ann Major's sizzling
stories featuring Honey, Midnight...and Innocence!

IN SEPTEMBER, YOU EXPERIENCED...

WILD HONEY Man of the Month
A clash of wills set the stage for an electrifying romance for
J. K. Cameron and Honey Wyatt.

IN NOVEMBER YOU ENJOYED...

WILD MIDNIGHT
Heat Up Your Winter
A bittersweet reunion turned into a once-in-a-lifetime adventure for
Lacy Douglas and Johnny Midnight.

AND IN FEBRUARY 1994, LOOK FOR...

WILD INNOCENCE Man of the Month
One man's return sets off a startling chain of events for
Innocence Lescuer and Raven Wyatt.

Let your wilder side take over with this exciting series—only from
Silhouette Desire!

SILHOUETTE®

Desire®

**COMING IN
FEBRUARY FROM
SILHOUETTE DESIRE...**

**SIX SINGLE GUYS GET A
BIG SURPRISE WHEN THEY FALL HARD
FOR THEIR MS. RIGHT!**

*Bachelor
Boys*

WILD INNOCENCE a *Man of the Month* by Ann Major
YESTERDAY'S OUTLAW by Raye Morgan
SEVEN YEAR ITCH by Peggy Moreland
TWILIGHT MAN by Karen Leabo
RICH GIRL, BAD BOY by Audra Adams
BLACK LACE AND LINEN by Susan Carroll

***THESE SIX SEXY BACHELORS WON'T
KNOW WHAT HITS THEM TILL
THE RING IS ON THEIR FINGER!***

SDBB

SILHOUETTE... Where Passion Lives

Don't miss these Silhouette favorites by some of our most distinguished authors! And now you can receive a discount by ordering two or more titles!

SD	#05772	FOUND FATHER by Justine Davis	$2.89 ☐
SD	#05783	DEVIL OR ANGEL by Audra Adams	$2.89 ☐
SD	#05786	QUICKSAND by Jennifer Greene	$2.89 ☐
SD	#05796	CAMERON by Beverly Barton	$2.99 ☐
IM	#07481	FIREBRAND by Paula Detmer Riggs	$3.39 ☐
IM	#07502	CLOUD MAN by Barbara Faith	$3.50 ☐
IM	#07505	HELL ON WHEELS by Naomi Horton	$3.50 ☐
IM	#07512	SWEET ANNIE'S PASS by Marilyn Pappano	$3.50 ☐
SE	#09791	THE CAT THAT LIVED ON PARK AVENUE by Tracy Sinclair	$3.39 ☐
SE	#09793	FULL OF GRACE by Ginna Ferris	$3.39 ☐
SE	#09822	WHEN SOMEBODY WANTS by Trisha Alexander	$3.50 ☐
SE	#09841	ON HER OWN by Pat Warren	$3.50 ☐
SR	#08866	PALACE CITY PRINCE by Arlene James	$2.69 ☐
SR	#08916	UNCLE DADDY by Kasey Michaels	$2.69 ☐
SR	#08948	MORE THAN YOU KNOW by Phyllis Halldorson	$2.75 ☐
SR	#08954	HERO IN DISGUISE by Stella Bagwell	$2.75 ☐
SS	#27006	NIGHT MIST by Helen R. Myers	$3.50 ☐
SS	#27010	IMMINENT THUNDER by Rachel Lee	$3.50 ☐
SS	#27015	FOOTSTEPS IN THE NIGHT by Lee Karr	$3.50 ☐
SS	#27020	DREAM A DEADLY DREAM by Allie Harrison	$3.50 ☐

(limited quantities available on certain titles)

AMOUNT	$	
DEDUCT: **10% DISCOUNT FOR 2+ BOOKS**	$	
POSTAGE & HANDLING	$	
($1.00 for one book, 50¢ for each additional)		
APPLICABLE TAXES*	$	
TOTAL PAYABLE	$	
(check or money order—please do not send cash)		

To order, complete this form and send it, along with a check or money order for the total above, payable to Silhouette Books, to: **In the U.S.:** 3010 Walden Avenue, P.O. Box 9077, Buffalo, NY 14269-9077; **In Canada:** P.O. Box 636, Fort Erie, Ontario, L2A 5X3.

Name: _____

Address: _____ City: _____

State/Prov.: _____ Zip/Postal Code: _____

*New York residents remit applicable sales taxes.
Canadian residents remit applicable GST and provincial taxes.   SBACK-JM

V Silhouette®